CERBERUS MC BOOK 10

BY MARIE JAMES

Copyright

Tug: Cerberus MC Book 9
Copyright © 2019 Marie James
Editing by Marie James Betas
EBooks are not transferrable. All rights are reserved. No part of this book may be used or reproduced in any manner without written permission, except in the case of brief quotations embodied in critical articles and reviews. The unauthorized reproduction or distribution of this copyrighted work is illegal. No part of this book may be scanned, uploaded, or distributed via the Internet or any other means, electronic or print, without the publisher's permission.

This book is a work of fiction. The names, characters, places, and incidents are products of the writer's imagination or have been used fictitiously and are not to be construed as real. Any resemblance to persons, living or dead, actual events, locale, or organizations is entirely coincidental.

Acknowledgments

Huge shout out this time around to the #1 man in my life! My dear, sweet husband, you are amazing! Thank you for making my dreams come true and supporting me relentlessly from day one. This wouldn't be possible it is wasn't for your support!

My amazing BETAs, you ladies are the absolute best! Laura, MaRanda, Brenda, Jamie, Michelle, and Jo thank you so much for the help on this book! Mary, you amaze me each and every time we work together! Thank you for your help and all of your support through this process!

Laura Watson! Thank you! You keep my head on right. I couldn't do this without you!

Another shout out to RRR Promotions and Natasha for helping get this book out into the world. As always you nailed it!

Readers, I can't even begin to tell you what you mean to me. Without you, I'd have no reason to write these books. Thanks for your continued support of the Cerberus MC!

Until next time!
~Marie James

Synopsis

The plans I made for my life didn't pan out.

I walked away from my best friend, my lover, the only man I could see spending my life with to make a career of being a Marine, but it didn't happen.

A car accident took him away from me before I realized the mistake I'd made.

Now, thirteen years later, I've met a woman and a man who makes everything seem ideal.

He's perfect in a familiar kind of way, and she's the kind of brand new you can't get enough of.

It's just my luck that one's a ghost and the other is my boss's daughter.

These plans may not pan out either.

This is NOT a paranormal romance

Tug is a standalone MMF novel in an interconnected series

Prologue

Tug

"I'm glad you came out tonight."

I smile and press my lips to the top of Max's head.

"Never doubt that I'll always be here for you," I remind him, not for the first time since we started whatever it is we're doing.

We haven't labeled it, doing so would require a level of reflection I won't allow myself. How do you even begin to understand having feelings for the boy you grew up with, especially when you're a boy yourself? So we haven't labeled it. I don't think there's a clear title to what we are. All I know is I love this boy with all my heart, and he feels the same for me.

The real pain comes from knowing that even though we feel this way about each other, it won't keep us from parting ways tomorrow. I'm heading into the Marine Corps, and he's going to stick around town and do what every Vazquez man in his family has done before him; he's going to work for his family.

"I'll consider going to college if you stay." His words are sad, most likely because we've had this conversation a million times before, and my answer never changes.

I know he's not destined for formal education, just as he knows the Corps is the only thing that will save me from my own father. Where his expects him to contribute to his family by way of working in their family-run shop; mine only sees me as a whipping boy, the person he turns on to blow off steam with his fists when he has a bad day. Every day is a bad day for my old man.

"You don't want to go to college," I remind him.

Max only graduated because I helped him with his classes all through high school, and even with my help, he had a couple of close calls. The computer and tech classes were the only ones he excelled at, but it's knowing he has to take all the other ones in college that will keep him away. He's a smooth talker with charisma like I've never seen before, but he knows he can't bullshit his way through college.

"But I want you to stay."

I sigh, pulling him closer to my chest. As much as I want to be annoyed with his insistent begging, internally, I wish there was an alternative solution. I'd love nothing more than to stay here with him, but my options are limited in this town.

"I can't stay."

"You can't be gay in the Marines, either. They'll kill you if they even suspect it."

"I'm not gay."

This is another conversation we've had countless times.

"You just got finished sucking me off," he says as if I need the reminder when his taste is still heavy on my tongue.

"And I told you before, you're the only guy I'm attracted to. You're the only man that gets me hard. No one is going to know about my history because I'm not going to do to others what I've been doing to you for the last year."

"But you won't write to me while you're gone."

It isn't a question. He knows better than to start this line of conversation again, but he's grasping at straws. I don't blame him. I always tell him no, but in actuality, I'm dying to say yes. Yes, I'll stay. Yes, I'll love him forever. Yes, I'll spend the rest of my life loving him no matter the consequences for coming out in our small little country town.

I've played the hard-ass for the last six months, ever since the recruiter came to school and offered me a life I never thought I could have.

We're best friends, but he knows once the sun comes up, I'm going into the Corps and not looking back. It makes me the biggest asshole that ever lived, but I'm walking away from everything, including him. As far as I see it, I have no other choice. If I stay, my dad will end up killing me. He's come close one too many times, and as much as I want to choose Max, I'm choosing myself this time. Selfishness comes easy for an only child, and I'm taking control of my life the only way I see fit.

"I'm still holding out hope that you'll come to your senses."

"Max," I grumble.

"I know," he interrupts before I can continue. "Just know that if you decide the Corps isn't for you, or if you just miss me too much, I'll be here for you. I can't imagine loving anyone the way I love you. I'll be here."

Four hours later, I leave him asleep in the treehouse in his backyard, hating that I never told him I loved him, too.

Three years later, I would be hit in the gut with the news that my best friend, my lover, the only person I could ever picture growing old with was dead. A car accident on rain-drenched roads had the power to take a life and leave me an empty shell.

The regret of walking away from him, from not being there for him will eat me alive.

Motion to my left draws my attention and if I were anywhere else, the sight of the woman on her knees, servicing a man sitting on the barstool right beside me would make me gasp. Here, it's expected, so I don't bother to pull my gaze from the way her lips spread wide to pull his girth deeper into her throat.

Her whimpers, when he presses too deep, hit me in the core. It also makes me want to find my own fun quicker than I normally would.

"Man, that's a sexy sight."

I grin before turning my head toward the man who just spoke.

"Yes, it is," I agree as we both turn our gazes back to the man just in time to see his face screw up in pleasure as his orgasm shoots down his friend's throat.

"I'm Carlos."

The man offers me his tanned hand, and out of courtesy, I take it to shake.

"Lilly," I tell him. "Pleasure to meet you."

"Hopefully, the pleasure will be for both of us."

There's an accented lilt to his voice, and it only makes his appeal grow tenfold. I love an exotic man, and there's something about Latin men that drives me insane. The black mask wrapped around his face makes me think of Zorro, and that also makes me want to know more about him.

"Wanna find a dark corner and get to know each other a little better?"

I know exactly what he's asking, but this isn't a normal club. I came here exactly for what he's offering.

I can't wait to get started.

Chapter 2

Tug

"The black band only means people can approach you for anything. It doesn't give them permission to touch or force you into anything you aren't comfortable doing," the man behind the counter explains as he fastens it to my wrist. "You can always say no to anything that is offered or requested. If you run into trouble, there are monitors spread throughout the club. Just look for the men in bright yellow shirts."

He skips the stamp on the back of my hand this time since this is my second time here.

"Have fun, my man."

I'm moving toward the heavy wooden door before he can even point me in that direction.

Music floods out, wrapping around me like a fist when I step inside the open room. Twenty feet in front of me a woman dances seductively in a cage. She's stark naked, and even though she has a smile on her face indicating that she's down for just about everything, the collar around her slender neck makes sure others keep their distance. A man dressed in a custom-cut suit watches her with pride as she moves her hips with the rhythm of the song playing in the background.

I've been to enough strip clubs that although I can appreciate her appeal, just a naked woman dancing doesn't even make my cock jerk.

It takes more these days for him to stand up and take notice, but in a place like this, even that doesn't take long. Deeper into the room a bed of plush pillows holds no less than five people, and the sight of the men and women in a free-for-all makes me pause to enjoy the show.

Leaning against one of the eight giant pillars in the room, I watch with rapt attention as one woman licks up and down the pussy of another while being hammered into by a burly guy. Both women moan from his powerful thrusts. One taking the brunt of his drives while the other is rewarded with the nudges of her mouth.

My cock, half-awake, jolts when another man positions himself behind the rooting guy. On pins and needles, I wait for the opportunist to be shoved away, but the aggression never comes. Rather, the first man slows his hips long enough for the new man to plant himself deep inside of him. Everyone groans in unison as the man, now in the middle, moves back and forth, effectively fucking and getting fucked at the same time.

"Jesus," a man whispers beside me, "I'd never have the ability to do that. Just look at him taking it."

I grin but don't turn my head in the direction of the man who is no doubt trying to lure me into a conversation. I didn't come here to talk. I just want to play a little, get off, and get back home.

I've already fielded five text messages from the guys back at the clubhouse wondering where I disappeared to. I explained that I needed a night away and turned my phone to silent. It's none of their business why I'm here tonight, and I certainly wasn't going to bother trying to explain that even though there is a plethora of women at the clubhouse willing to jump on my dick, I was missing something. I've been unhappy sexually for a very long time, and tonight my only plan is to revisit the only reason I can think of that could be causing it.

"I bet I could fuck like that guy, but don't think I'd enjoy taking it," the man continues even though I've given him no indication that I want to continue to engage with him.

"Too bad," I purr, finally turning to look him in the eye. With one hand gripping his hip and the other reaching up to rub my finger over his bottom lip, I grin down at him. "I'd love nothing more than to fuck that tight ass of yours."

His eyes widen before his mouth releases a quick squeak. He's gone a second later, and I don't bother holding in my chuckle.

"If you're looking for an ass to fuck, there's a couple in the glass room. He's wearing a blue band, and she's got on a green one." The monitor is gone as soon as the words leave his mouth.

Blue indicates gay sex; alternatively, pink is a request for girl-on-girl action. Green stands for group sex which also symbolizes that the wearer is okay with same-sex action.

I ponder on it for a while as I make my way to the bar, ordering both of my drinks in one go instead of wasting time nursing one before ordering the other. I drop a twenty in the tip jar as both of my drinks are delivered, unceremoniously tossing both of them back without even bothering to taste them.

"Most people make 'em last since they only get two."

I grin at the bartender, allowing my eyes to sweep down his chest. He grunts as I look at the name tag pinned to his thin cotton shirt.

"Well, Dylan," my eyes find his again, "I don't like wasting time."

"That so?" He grins at me, and this is what fully wakes up my cock. "You just like to dig in and go for it, huh?"

"Exactly."

I stand a little taller when his eyes rove over my body.

"If you stick around later, I may put that little black band of yours to work." Dominance laces his tone, and surprisingly, I don't find myself turned off by it. "I get off at two. Maybe I'll see you around."

He taps his knuckles on the bar top twice before moving down a few feet to fill another man's order. Without his stare on me and the suggestive pull of his mouth, cold chills swarm my body. I've never, not once in my entire life flirted with another man other than—

"No," I hiss, refusing to acknowledge the pain deep in my gut from the time right before I joined the Marines.

With laser focus, I make my way across the open floor plan toward the rooms in the back. The glass room suggested by the monitor isn't hard to find, and the couple on the bed are so enthralled with each other that they don't pay any attention to the dozen or so people crowded around the glass watching them. They aren't putting on a show particularly. They're just enjoying pleasuring each other.

The woman, on all fours over the man, is not only in prime position to take the man's cock, but she's also splayed open as her cunt is licked and nipped by the man under her.

Circles are cut out of the glass about two feet from the ceiling allowing every one of us on this side of the partition to hear their moans and gasps. One man beside me strokes himself without a care in the world while another man is thrusting his fingers deep into the drenched pussy of a woman beside him.

My cock is rock hard, but it's not just him or her, it's both of them together. It's the way he clenches his ass to drive his cock deeper in her throat and the sight of his wet fingers when he pulls them back before sliding them back inside of her.

When he plunges his pussy-coated thumb in her ass, she releases his erection with a loud moan, and the sight of her neck arched in pleasure makes me want to step inside and join but interrupting their scene uninvited would be against the rules.

As if she could read my thoughts, her butterfly mask turns in my direction. She points at me as her mouth opens on another groan. She comes, shaking violently as her finger crooks in invitation.

I point to my chest, needing to make sure before stepping around the glass.

She nods with a salacious hitch of her lips, and her smile only grows wider when she realizes I'm taking her up on her offer.

"Hey, handsome," the man on the bed says as I stand to the side and begin to undress. "Lilly, won't you help me make our new guest more comfortable?"

Her legs seem weak as she climbs off the man, no doubt the aftereffects from the orgasm she just had. Both bite their lips as they close the distance between us, and my skin itches in anticipation. It's been so long since I've been touched by a man, but the second his fingers open my belt and flick the button on my jeans, I know this is exactly what I've been missing. Women are amazing, and I can't imagine going through life without a pussy to eat and fuck, but the man shoving my jeans down and running a teasing finger on the underside of my balls seems to fit in my fucked-up puzzle as well.

"Look how hot he is for us, butterfly."

Butterfly/Lilly still hasn't released her lip from between her teeth as her fingers toy with the hem of my t-shirt. I lift my arms, crouching lower so she can pull it over my head, all the while using the toe of one boot to push the other off my foot. The second one is harder to deal with, but I manage. By the time my jeans are around my ankles, my feet are free to kick the denim away.

They both lean back on their haunches and admire the sight before them. My skin tingles under their perusal, but no one speaks. The silence is loud enough that the sound of a man climaxing can be heard on the other side of the glass. My fists clench and open rhythmically as I fight the urge to run. Exploring this side of me is one thing; doing it while on display is a totally different situation.

"I-I can't—"

"You better get in there and wrap your mouth around that glorious cock before he bolts," the grinning man suggests.

"You do it." My eyes widen when my thoughts are spoken out loud rather than staying in my head as I'd planned.

"Me?" The man points to his chest, black mask raising an inch or so when his eyebrows shoot up.

"You," I whisper. "I mean if you want to."

I add the last part aware that although he's wearing a blue band which clearly indicates he's down for this exact thing, just like I do, he too has the right to refuse anything at any point.

"My pleasure," he purrs with the slightest hint of an accent. The inflection is just enough that when I close my eyes just as he's closing his mouth over my cockhead, I can imagine it's Max on the bed taking me inside.

"Fuck," I grunt when he wastes no time taking me to the back of his throat. He swallows with me lodged deep, and the sensation of his throat closing around me is almost enough to send me over the edge.

"Why don't you join us on the bed?" The sultry voice of the woman is like a siren's call. It fills my blood, and without thought, I obey her request.

The man doesn't seem to mind when I pull from his mouth and reach for her. As they guide me to lay on my back in the center of the bed, I position her glistening cunt over my mouth. He wastes no time taking me back in his throat.

"This is the hottest thing I've ever seen," she pants, her hips rocking back and forth over my tongue.

Fuck, I love a woman who isn't afraid to take her own pleasure, to do what feels right without the worry of upsetting her partner.

She rides my face to another orgasm, shuddering against my mouth, her hips still swiveling against my tongue as she wrings every second of pleasure she can manage from the situation.

I'm certain she's going to lift off me and crash to the bed, but instead, she leans forward taking my cock into her mouth while our bedmate focuses his attention on my nuts.

"I need to fuck," I grunt, and the sight I witnessed earlier on the bed of pillows in the main room comes to mind. There would be nothing hotter than this man sliding his dick into her while I thrust into him. "Who's it going to be?"

I leave the options open as I ask because this was their party, and I'm merely a secondary invite. As far as I know, they could ask me to leave.

"I need a couple of minutes before I'm ready for more," the woman says as she climbs off me, and her teeth dig into her lower lip for a long moment before she speaks again. Her sultry voice is a low whisper, and I imagine she's keeping it low to keep it personal even as the people on the other side of the glass strain to hear. "I'd love to see you two fuck. I've never been this close to that kind of action before."

"Your wish, Lilly, is our command."

The man moves to grab a condom and a single-use packet of lube from the fishbowl on a side table, and I'm seconds away from explaining that this isn't going to happen the way he's planning when he opens the condom and turns to roll it down my dick.

"Calm down," he urges as he rolls the latex down my dick. "You don't seem like the type that will stick his ass in the air for me."

"Carlos," Lilly chides with a chuckle, "you never know, he could love getting fucked in the ass. I know I do."

"I don't," I grunt. I ignore the way my cock jerks. It's either the thought of letting someone inside of me that way for the first time or the knowledge that Lilly isn't a stranger to getting drilled there. I'm going with the latter because the former isn't something I'm going to address tonight.

Carlos pulls his head back as if he's been slapped, and I'm immediately thankful for the mask covering my face. It doesn't keep his dark brown eyes from searching every other feature on display, however.

"We going to do this?" I ask when it doesn't seem like he's going to stop staring anytime soon.

"Have you ever done this before?"

Without answering, I hold my hand out for the lube packet. Like magic, it's already open and instead of handing me the packet, he squeezes the gel out on the tips of my index and middle finger. Lilly shifts to the side as he lays flat on his back.

My movements stutter, his position almost too intimate for what I had planned. Fucking him face to face would be too much for me to handle.

"Just while you prep me," he says as if he's answering a question that wasn't asked. "Here, Lilly, hold this leg."

She pushes against Carlos's thigh, spreading him for me, and my fucking mouth waters. I want to suck his dick while my fingers prepare him to take my cock, but the sight isn't only appealing to me because Lilly leans forward and takes him in her mouth.

"So fucking hot," I mutter more to myself than my new friends as I lean in and tease his ass with my greased up fingers.

With her bent over, I notice for the first time a pink, purple, and blue butterfly tattoo on her ass. I grin at the sight of it.

"Quit teasing," Carlos gasps just before his hand reaches down to grab my wrist. "Fuck me with them."

His words make me freeze. I've heard that exact phrase a dozen times a lifetime ago.

"I can help," Lilly says as she grabs the lube packet from the bed and coats her own fingers. "How about one of each?"

She clasps my hand, folding down all but one finger, and guides both of our fingers into Carlos's slick entrance. All I can do is allow it to happen as I watch his eyes. His lips part on a moan as he takes part of me and part of her inside of him.

Before long, the memories trying to force their way into my head turn to vapor as the need for sex fills every nook and cranny of this room.

The condom glistens as my cock tests the strength of the latex when Carlos, well prepared and begging for more, turns to his side. He instructs Lilly to roll a rubber down his own dick. The second the condom is in place, he guides her to her own side, lifts her top leg, and slams inside of her. He moans his euphoria, and the sound makes me wish I could slide inside of her as well. When his top leg lifts and the sight of his cock plowing into her hits my eyes, I waste no time lying behind him and getting into position. The sex gods must be listening tonight because I'm somehow managing to get exactly what I came here for.

"Oh, God," Carlos mutters when I breach him. The first clench of his ass around me makes me drive deeper. "Go slow. Fuck, you're bigger than you look."

I grip his hip as I slowly inch forward. It's too much too soon, and he shifts his hips forward, but his escape is Lilly's pleasure as he drives deeper in her.

"I won't last," I warn as my hips shift back a few inches only to drive forward twice as far.

"Me either," Carlos pants.

"Play with her clit," I instruct, and Carlos moves into action. "You're so fucking tight."

"Been a while," he confesses just before shifting his hips back, testing the depth of my cock.

"Just like that," I praise, holding my own hips static as he finds a rhythm that has all of us moaning in pleasure.

Lilly comes like a queen, moaning her release which sets Carlos off. Her clenching pussy is matched in kind with the pulses of his own orgasm, and the strength of his release rips mine from me as well.

I think we lay there for what seems like hours before Lilly finally pulls free. It takes a minute or so longer before either Carlos or I move.

Lilly and Carlos discuss returning in two weeks for more playtime as we all get dressed. I make a point to be careful with my mask. As much fun as I had with these two, I still don't want anyone to see my face.

When the monitors walk around ten minutes later, they let everyone know that two is fast approaching and no masks are allowed.

I don't know who got out of there faster, Lilly or me.

Chapter 3

Jasmine

"As I said at the beginning of class, all the resources you need are listed online."

I don't bother to look over at Wesley as he trails along beside me as I exit the humanities building.

"That list only goes to another list of resources in the library," he whines. "It just means it's twice the work."

"And such is the life of a college student." I bite the inside of my lip to keep from smiling at the incredulous huff that escapes his lips.

"I was hoping for a more hands-on approach to this class."

The innuendo is clear as day as I push out of the main doors toward the parking lot.

"That list of resources is all you need."

"Maybe you offer tutoring. Like after-hours?" When I look over at him, his eyebrows are wagging up and down. He's handsome, for a kid that is. No older than eighteen, nineteen at the most, Wesley grins at me as if the smirk on his lips would entice me into some sort of teacher-fucks-student situation that would not only get me fired but also doesn't appeal to me at all. That's the problem with college boys. They haven't managed to grow the brains they need to score anything other than young girls who don't know any better. He doesn't have a clue what I'd need, and his skill set, seemingly resting solely on that silly grin on his too-full lips, is probably the strongest thing the child has in his arsenal.

"Sorry, Wesley, the resources provided are the only ones I can offer. Maybe get with a peer tutor or another student who understands the material better from class. I don't know how things worked for you in high school, but you're going to have to put in the hours if you want to pass my class."

His feet stop, and I feel the heat of his agitated gaze on my back as I make my way toward my car.

"Bitch," he mutters behind my back.

I don't bother to turn around. Getting into a power struggle in the middle of the college parking lot won't do me any good, but I do file his name away for later, so I can grade his next assignment with a heavier hand. Such is the power of the college professor. I don't even understand his problem. Intro to Philosophy isn't a hard class. With minimal skills in critical thinking and the ability to argue his way out of a paper bag, he should be able to pull a solid B easily.

"Boys," I mutter as I climb inside of my car.

No doubt Wesley has nothing on the two men I spent the evening with two weeks ago. There was something about their strong muscles, fearless needs, and ability to please each other that will leave me wanting whenever I'm with another man.

My choice to go to *Hale-ish Retreat and Spa* has been my best decision to date. Sexually, I have never had such an experience. Although tonight is another masquerade night, I'm unable to make it. I've been tasked with helping create the menu for Thanksgiving dinner, which just happens to be less than a week away. It's one of the downfalls of being the oldest 'kid' in the group.

A good thing, however, is that Delilah, Ivy, Griffin, and Lawson are flying in later this evening. I haven't seen them since before the semester began, although I've spent some time with Camryn and Samson during the last couple of months.

Samson used to be one of those boys that thought he could rule the world with a well-placed smirk, but he learned quickly that his love interest, an obstetrical surgical resident at the hospital, wasn't playing into that nonsense. Most boys, however, don't grow up that fast. They don't have the ability to adapt and change when the woman they want isn't interested in the package they present the first time. It reeks of immaturity and narcissism.

My ringing cell phone jolts me from the memories I've been drowning myself in since I left the club. I press the answer button on my car screen and smile, waiting for my sister to speak.

"Jasmine? Are you there?"

"I'm here," I answer. "How are you?"

"Don't give me that how are you mess. You've been avoiding me for two weeks."

"I have not," I argue.

I totally have been.

"Liar!" She's animated, and I already know what she wants to talk about, hence the reason I haven't answered any of her texts or emails. "Tell me how it went."

"School is great. There are a couple of lazy kids who don't want to do the work, but other than that I think it's going to be a successful semes—"

"Don't give me that shit. You know exactly what I'm asking about, and it certainly isn't about classes. I go to school all damn day. I don't want to talk about it when I call."

"Mom and Dad are great. They wish you were able to make it home for the holidays, but they understand that one trip a year is the most they're going to get. I bet Oxford is gorgeous when it snows. Is there snow there yet?"

She huffs, remaining silent for several minutes. If it weren't for the tracker keeping time of our call, I'd think she hung up on me.

"Soph?"

She doesn't answer.

"Sophia Gayle Anderson, I'm not discussing my sex life with you."

She huffs again.

"It's not appropriate."

"Like covering for you when you were in high school wasn't appropriate?"

"One time!" I hiss. "You lied to them for me once."

"You were still sneaking out to meet a boy."

"To work on that project for film class. You knew we couldn't do those graveyard scenes during the daytime. Dad was being a jerk for not letting me go with the others in the class."

Thirty and clearly still bitter about it.

"Don't get testy." She chuckles. "It's not my fault you never wanted to sneak out for the good stuff."

"You say that like you have a history with it."

One thing I know about my little sister is that if you can manage to get her to talk about herself, all intention of speaking about what she wanted to talk about will fly out the window.

"I crawled out of my bedroom window countless times. I always felt sorry for those living on Cerberus property. It was nearly impossible to get away unnoticed from there. But," she emphasizes the T, "I didn't call to talk about me. I want to know how it went at the club."

"The club?"

"Don't play coy with me. Gigi told me you were going."

"Gigi has a big mouth," I grumble. "What are the boys like there? I bet it's hard to keep from swooning when they talk. God, I love a good accent."

"One, no one says swoon, and two, all the boys here are idiots. Accents or not, they're just as stupid as American boys. Thinking a couple of grins are enough to get girls in bed. So stupid."

I smile wide, remembering my earlier thoughts.

"You just need to wait for the right guy to come along."

"Says the woman who frequents sex clubs," she mutters.

"You need to stop believing everything you hear."

"So, don't pay attention to the truth?" I don't answer her. I refuse to fall into one of her conversational traps. "When I come home for the wedding and Christmas, I want you to take me."

"Fat fucking chance. You're not old enough."

"Twenty-one is old enough," she counters.

Damn it. She has me there.

"That's not something I'm ever going to do for you."

"I can get Gigi to take me then."

"She won't go without Jameson, and he wouldn't allow it. Plus, he could end up seeing you naked or something."

"Don't threaten me with a good time."

I hear the laughter in her voice, and I have to admit, Jameson is one sexy man. He's nothing like the vapid teens I'm tasked with trying to educate every day.

"You really won't take me?"

"I don't think it's the kind of place sisters should experience together." That's the nicest response I can manage. There's not one second of watching my sister get freaky in a sex club that entices me. I imagine that if I think about it long enough, I'd manage to hate the idea of sex clubs altogether.

"But you go all the time."

"So, do as I say not as I do."

"You sound exactly like Mom," she complains.

"She's a wise woman."

"I'm going to tell her you said that," Sophia teases. I'm just grateful she seems to have given up on begging me about going to the club together.

My laugh accompanies me as I pull into the parking lot of my apartment.

"I'm going to miss you at Thanksgiving dinner."

"I wish I could be there." Sadness fills her tone, and it makes me wish I could reach my arms through the phone and hug her.

I was eight, almost nine when my half-sister Makayla and her new husband Dominic adopted me. I was almost ten by the time Sophia came along, but that just meant that I was old enough to help take care of her. I used to imagine Sophia being my own daughter, and I've always felt a sense of motherly duty over her. She wasn't very impressed with my 'mothering' when she got into her teen years, and she always let me know that I was crossing a boundary. Things have settled in that sense since she graduated high school, but I've always wondered if her reason for moving clear across the globe to go to college in the United Kingdom was because she was tired of being watched over by three parents.

"I love you," I tell her.

"Love you, too. Have some banana pudding for me."

"You got it," I agree.

All I have planned for the day is getting changed, heading to the clubhouse to work on the holiday menu, and trying not to regret missing a night at the club.

By the time I make it across town, everyone from Rhode Island has already arrived. Boisterous laughter and affection are thick when I open the front door to the clubhouse. The family that raised me accepted me immediately as one of their own greets me when I make my way to the kitchen.

The Cerberus guys must be out of town because my dad, Uncle Diego, Dustin, Jaxon, and Rob, along with some of the younger generation males are the only ones around.

"Where's your crew at?" I ask Uncle Diego when he pulls me into a hug.

"They'll be home in time for the holiday," he assures me before releasing me and urging me into his wife's direction.

I take every hug they offer, even though I saw them only a few days ago. Going from this chaos to college where there seemed to never be a second alone, to living alone has been more of a struggle than I'd admit to anyone out loud. It's why I spend so much of my free time here at the clubhouse or at my parents' house.

"I'm glad you're here," Delilah says with a squeal as she wraps her arms around me. "You can help me finalize plans for the wedding!"

I smile at her as she releases me. "I'm here to help."

The laughter and voices grow louder as each person tries to be heard over the din created by so many people in the same area. It doesn't get any better than this.

Chapter 4

Tug

Pulling up outside of *Hale-ish*, the sight of another bike in the lot has me second-guessing my plans, but upon further inspection, it isn't one I recognize, so the likelihood of it being someone I know is slim.

"Another black band tonight?" the bouncer asks when I check in at the desk.

"Please." I offer my wrist for him to wrap the dark band around it and then waste no time pushing the wooden door open so I can join the party.

I'm a little earlier than I was four weeks ago with the hope that my two play partners from the last time haven't found someone else to entertain them for the night. My cock has been hard for weeks with the memories, and I stroked it twice before leaving the clubhouse with the mere anticipation of seeing them again.

As I step up to the bar, Dylan pours my two drinks without having to ask for them. It's busier, but I imagine people are using their yearly vacation days before they expire January first. The handsome bartender winks at me before turning to help another customer, so without the opportunity to engage with him again, I turn around and face the room.

People aren't wasting any time, as I don't imagine they ever do while they're here. This is nothing like a regular bar or club. The bands on our wrists help skip the small talk, and since everyone is here to get off, the selection process is all that's left.

The monarch face mask catches my eye, but it is a dull reflection of the colorful tattoo I admired on her ass weeks ago. A man is already at her side, but as if she can feel my eyes on her, she turns her head in my direction. Next, the Zorro look-alike turns his head as well. A small grin spreads across his face, but even from here I can tell he isn't as happy as she is to see me.

I turn up each of my drinks, one after the other, before leaving the empty glasses on the bar and walking toward them. If they both don't want to play, that's fine, too. There are dozens of other people here who can assist in getting me off. Being rejected by him would suck, but I'm a big boy. I refuse to let it ruin my night.

"Hey there," Lilly purrs as I step closer.

Reaching down, I lift her hand, brushing my lips across the top.

"Smooth," she says with a chuckle.

"Carlos," I greet with a nod.

"You never told us your name," she prods when the man beside her and I just lock eyes with each other.

"You can call me King," I suggest.

It isn't far from the truth. I was born Kingston Jacks. My nickname was given in boot camp, and it just kind of stuck. I'd much rather be called Tug, but I also don't want to mix my business with Cerberus with my pleasure here.

"King," Carlos says as if he's testing out the words in his mouth.

His throat works on a swallow as he rubs his lips together.

"Would you like to join us, King?" Lilly asks, patting the empty spot on her side opposite of Carlos.

The second man clears his throat, but I ignore him. He enjoyed what we did, came too hard last time we played to be too upset that I'm encroaching on their night once again.

Taking my spot beside Lilly, I turn my eyes to the activities of the room. Against the far wall, a petite brunette is getting one hell of a spanking. Her upturned ass is striped with welts as the man beside her with the cane shows no signs of stopping. I'd be concerned that he's taking it too far if it wasn't for the way her pussy is glistening in the low lights.

"I admire women like that." Lilly's words are breathless as she too turns to watch the show. "I'd never be brave enough to do that."

"You'd be surprised what you're into if you just give it a try," Carlos says.

My muscles stiffen at his words, the similar echo from my past once again rearing its head.

"I tried it in a club in Albuquerque. It seems pain isn't my thing." She shifts beside me. "But I have to admit that watching makes me hot."

"Maybe you had the wrong partner," I insist, turning my attention from the now orgasming woman back to her. "We can try it here if you want. A little light spanking, maybe?"

Her white teeth once again dig into her lower lip as she mulls over the prospect.

"Imagine how much fun it would be. King can spank that amazing ass of yours while I fuck you with my fingers. How does that sound?" Carlos's fingers trail up the inside of her thigh, and as he reaches the short hem of her dress, she widens them just slightly.

Her eyes dart between us, but she doesn't verbally deny what is being offered. I don't like anyone directing my activities, but I can admit that his suggestion is beyond appealing.

"What do you say?" I prod, mimicking his action and running my fingers up her other thigh.

"We can try," she agrees, and a second later she has one leg draped over my lap and the other over Carlos', her pussy on display and easily accessible.

"No panties?" Carlos whispers against her neck as his fingers toy with her naked flesh.

"Naughty girl," I chide as I slide mine along his.

As if we've choreographed the move, each one of us slides a finger inside of her. The walls of her cunt ripple along our fingers, and it's clear now why Carlos came so fast weeks ago. Her pussy is tight, and oh so fucking hot.

"I-I ch-changed my clothes when I got to town. I didn't think panties were necessary."

"I like your style," I praise as I use my free hand to pull down the top of her slinky shirt. "No bra either?"

"Mmm," Carlos moans as his mouth finds one of her nipples.

"I agree." Not to be outdone, I wrap my lips around the other.

"I thought you were g-going to spank me," Lilly whispers.

"Anxious, are we?" Carlos says after releasing her breast with a pop.

His finger presses deeper alongside mine, and it only makes her whimper more. My cock is more than interested in what's going on, but when he lifts her heavy breast toward my mouth in offering, my entire body is on board. Neither one of us is taking what we need from her. We're sharing every aspect of this encounter. It's something I've never had before, and something I know I'm going to crave from now on.

"She's ready for you, King," Carlos pants.

He can feel the way her pussy is quivering, just like I can. When he nods, the unspoken cue to not let her come just yet, we simultaneously pull our fingers from her drenched core.

"Why did you stop?"

The only answer I give her is pressing my wet fingers to her mouth. Likewise, Carlos presses his against mine, his eyes growing heavy when both of us suck our offerings clean.

"Are you as good at sucking cock?"

His question makes me feel like an ass. Four weeks ago, I took everything offered to me. I accepted his blow job, accepted her pussy on my mouth, but I never offered to return the favor to him. I vow to change that before this night is over.

"You'll find out soon enough," I offer as I grab Lilly by the arms and lift her onto my lap. Not as coordinated as Carlos and I had been previously, she wiggles oddly before I can settle her face down with her abdomen resting on my thighs.

Carlos lifts her skirt, gripping the globes of her spectacular ass and spreading her cheeks. The dewy pink lips of her pussy make my mouth water, but I'm in no position to do anything about it. Carlos is the lucky bastard who gets to lean forward and tongue fuck both of her entrances like a greedy bastard.

"Are you enjoying that?" I ask before lifting my hand.

Lilly yelps when I slap the meat of one ass cheek, but it turns into a long-suffering groan as Carlos works his magical tongue into her depths. We discussed him fingering her while I swatted her ass, but clearly, the man can improvise like a champ.

"More," she begs after my third strike. "Harder."

The sight of my handprint on both sides of her ass has my cock throbbing in my jeans, but I give the woman what she wants. All it takes is two more hits to her ass, and she's coming on Carlos's mouth as he eats her like the man has been starved for a decade.

She's mewling like a kitten as she comes down from her high, but when Carlos lifts his face from her pleased snatch, it's the wetness on his lips that makes me hungry. Without a word, I reach up and cup the back of his neck. Much to my surprise, he doesn't fight me when I grip him harder and yank his mouth to mine. It's only my third time in the damn place, and I'm already breaking one of my hard-fast rules. I told myself *no kissing*. The act is too intimate, and it gives your play partners the wrong idea.

Carlos groans in my mouth when my tongue pushes past his lips to tangle with his own. Although it's been thirteen years since my lips have been on another man's mouth, it's like a day hasn't gone by since that last kiss I shared with Max. My throat burns with the memory, but it's impossible to pull my mouth from Carlos.

"That's the hottest fucking thing I've ever seen."

Carlos chuckles when we finally break apart. His eyes turn to the woman in my lap that has managed to turn facing up while I was lost in this man. My eyes stay on him as if I'm entranced at the sight of his dark brown orbs and the pieces of his face hidden behind his mask.

"If that's the case, you need to get out more often," Carlos tells Lilly.

"I can think of something else that's super-hot." Lilly is once again nibbling on her lower lip.

I reach up and tug the abused flesh from her teeth. "What do you want?"

"I think you promised Carlos a blow job," she says after long consideration.

"I did," I agree. "Is that what you want to see?"

She nods, and I'm more than willing to give the lady what she wants, but Carlos has a different idea of where this night is going. When I stand and reach for his belt, he shifts us so I'm the one sitting on the settee and he's on his knees working open my fly.

Chapter 5

Max

How is it possible after all this time this man still smells the same, still makes the same sounds when he comes? How do his lips still taste the same when thirteen years ago we spent our time in each other's arms not sipping whiskey and tag-teaming a woman?

I suspected weeks ago that he was my long-lost friend, but when he told us to call him King tonight, it clinched it for me. The thought of him hitting his knees to suck me off is enough to make me come in my jeans. There's no way I can let him get his lips around me. The embarrassment alone is enough to make me want to bolt.

Although the last complication I need right now is getting him off, it's like we're seventeen all over again, and my ability to resist him then was nil. Now? After over a decade without contact? There's no way I can refuse him.

Once his cock is free from its denim confines, I swipe my tongue over the tip, tentatively tasting him all the while trembling as I try not to give in to my instincts and suck him down my throat.

"Oh, fuck," Kingston moans as I tease that triangle on the underside of his meaty cock.

His hands are rougher than I remember when they grip my neck, but I'm sure that comes from his years in the Corps. I love the addition of his fingers tangled in my hair as he guides my mouth over his cock. That hasn't changed either. Even when we were younger, he was a little aggressive. It's only multiplied now. He grunts when I take him to the back of my throat. I know I need to get him off quickly, so maybe he'll leave so I can continue to woo Lilly, aka Jasmine Anderson, niece to Diego Anderson, the Cerberus MC president.

I bet the man with his cock in my mouth doesn't even have a clue that he's been servicing an MC princess. Her station isn't a concern for him, but it means everything to me, and twice now he's interfered.

I'm torn between letting him know who I am and hoping I won't be discovered. The teenager in me misses my best friend, but the grown man I am now has more complications than I can count and coming clean with Kingston Jacks would only add to my overburdened pile. Not to mention a wrench in my plans for Cerberus.

"So fucking good," Kingston groans.

His nuts begin to seize, but I'm not done with him yet. This may be the last time I'm awarded this opportunity, so I pull down on his sack as I pop my mouth off his cock. He hisses in frustration, but I only offer him a wink.

His fingers grip my hair tighter, urging me to lower my mouth back over his dick, but I merely swipe lazy kisses up and down his shaft and tongue his nuts. Spit has seeped down his balls, pooling at his taint and even lower. The shadows bouncing around the club don't give me the ability to see very well, but I'm more than able to conjure the sight of his asshole from memory.

Looking up at him, I kiss the tip of his cock as my fingers on his nuts sink lower. There's a warning in his eyes, but I ignore it.

"One little finger won't hurt. Promise." I said the very same thing years ago, the first night he relented and let me tease him there.

"Jesus," he pants, but the subtle nod of his head is all the permission I need.

As if she's no longer an active participant but just a voyeur in our little world, Lilly merely watches from the sidelines as I please him. She's turned on, the warm scent of her arousal has been growing stronger with each second I've spent on my knees, having doubled since I made her come.

"Feel good?"

His head shakes back and forth, and I know I'm pushing my limits. He has to remember the similarities from when we were teens to now, and it makes me want to push all the boundaries, the pull of having him here again is too much for me to stop.

"I think I'm going crazy," he whispers as he slams his eyes closed.

His legs are trembling now, but it's the sight of a single tear pooling on his eyelash that makes me reevaluate and take stock.

I'm torturing him, not only with my mouth but with my words. That wasn't my intention. I wanted to please him. I wanted him to remember me, so sure I was long forgotten, but clearly, that isn't the case.

"Fuck," he groans just as my finger brushes over his prostate.

The tear falls, and I'm so enthralled by it rolling from under his mask and down his cheek that I barely get my mouth over his cock before he explodes. Jet after jet of his salty release paints my tongue, and it's my turn to shed a tear. His taste familiar, but at the same time different. It's more manly, more addictive than it was years ago.

His fingers toy softly, gratefully on the side of my face, exactly like they did when we were younger as he regains his composure. The rough texture is new, but the sentiment is the same. The lights from the raised platform in the center of the room dance in his steel-gray eyes as he looks down at me.

"You can't even imagine how turned on I am right now," Lilly says, breaking into our stolen moment.

"I can smell your dripping pussy from here, butterfly," I tell her as I raise to my feet. Pulling my eyes from Kingston is nearly impossible, but I manage somehow. "What do you want?"

"I just need to get fucked." Her hand clamps over her lips, but not before a gasp escapes her lips.

I chuckle at her embarrassment.

"Tell me what you really need," I joke, but my fingers are working open my own fly as her cheeks turn pink. "Is it this?"

With a firm hand around the base of my cock, I point it in her direction.

"Yes," she purrs, her eyes focused on my cock. "I think that's just the thing."

"Do you want King to suck your nipples and play with your clit while you ride my cock?"

She gives me an enthusiastic nod, so I reach for a condom on the side table and sit right next to my old friend. He's stiff beside me, no doubt a little embarrassed and wondering if either of us saw that tear trickle down his cheek.

I can't focus on him for long because Lilly/Jasmine is pulling her skirt and top off without preamble before straddling my hips.

"Turn around," I urge with my hands on her hips. "I want everyone in the club to see what they can't have."

Settling her into a reverse cowgirl position, I angle my cock upward, so she can settle down over it. She doesn't waste any time grabbing Kingston by his neck and pulling his mouth toward her tits. His hand skates over my naked thigh before trailing up hers in search of her clit.

She moans when he makes initial contact, but I don't miss the brush of his fingers over my own sack as I ram inside of her.

"Jesus, baby. You're the tightest thing I've ever felt." It's a lie. Kingston's ass is the tightest thing I've ever felt, which was the exact same thing I told him the first time he let me finger-fuck him there. Her delectable pussy is a close second, though. "That's it. Let me fill you up."

She's whimpering, bouncing down on my dick like she's gone mad, but it's Kingston who draws most of my attention. I can feel his fingers still toying with her pussy, but his eyes are on mine, staring holes into me and trying to reconcile what he's known as truth for the last decade.

"Bite her nipple," I command, if anything to get those gorgeous eyes off me.

Thankfully, he obeys, and Lilly is so wound up from watching me finger-fuck Kingston's ass and suck him off that she's already on edge. Honestly, that makes two of us.

I start coming at the first clench of her greedy cunt, and I'm still blasting in the condom when she sinks down, replete and exhausted.

She's boneless when I finally manage to regain enough strength in my arms to lift her off my dick. Pressing a kiss to her forehead, I stand from the settee.

"I'll be back in a few minutes," I promise before walking away.

The bathroom and a few moments of silence are calling my name, and I need to answer that instead of giving in to the urge to pull my mask from my face and remind Kingston just how good we are together.

My plans and the life of someone I love dearly are in the balance, and even my love for the man who left me crying the day he joined the Marine Corps isn't enough to keep me from carrying through with why I'm here in the first place.

Chapter 6

Tug

Nothing makes sense.

With the frenzied exhilaration of my orgasm waning, my head once again becomes a clusterfuck. The added sight of watching Carlos walk away has me frazzled beyond belief.

"You're not bolting away, too, are you?" Lilly grabs at my arm, but I move too fast for her to catch me.

"I'll be right back," I promise, but I know the assurance is a lie.

After what I think I'm going to find when I confront Carlos, I don't think I'll be able to do much of anything.

It takes forever weaving through the crowd that has only grown since I settled on the sofa with Lilly and Carlos.

Carlos.

What a fucking crock of bullshit.

My steps falter as I reach the men's room, my hand wavering over the door pull, terrified of finding out the truth which means so much of my life over the last ten years has been a lie, one bred of deceit of the worst kind.

Am I letting myself hope when there isn't any hope to be found?

Am I losing my mind?

Have ghosts from my past finally managed to catch up with me, prepared to torture me for the things I've done for my country? For things I did before I really became a man?

My own penchant for selfishness makes the decision for me as I grip the door handle and pull the door open.

I'm welcomed by an empty space filled with more luxury than one would expect to find in a bathroom. It leaves me wondering if Carlos was lying about hitting the head just to get away from us.

His words, the way he approached sucking my dick, and the taunting look in his eyes was all too reminiscent to the way things were all those years ago.

A commode flushes, letting me know I'm in fact not alone in the room, so I wait for the stall to open. Carlos steps out of the stall. If he's surprised to see me in here with him, the evidence isn't reflected on his handsome face.

"Hey, man," he says as he walks to the sink to wash his hands. "Had a good time tonight."

The accent, lighter and more refined than I remember from my teen years has me second-guessing myself once again. The possibility that I'm in the same room with the man who has haunted my thoughts for as long as I can remember isn't possible. *Right?*

His shoulders are broader, legs thicker. He seems taller, but I grew another three inches my first year in the Corps, so it wouldn't be farfetched that he, too, grew after we last saw each other.

"You remind me of someone I used to know," I blurt, unsure of how to approach this situation.

I'm torn between looking like a fool by ripping off his mask to learn the truth and walking away in desperate need for mental health services.

"I get that a lot," he says as he turns off the faucet and reaches for paper towels.

"Take off your mask," I demand, unable to reach out to him myself.

"That would be breaking the rules." He doesn't bother looking at me as he dries his hands, tossing the waste in the trash.

"I'm not one for rules."

He mutters something that sounds eerily close to, "You never were."

It drives me into action, forcing me to reach for the black fabric on his face, but with agile speed, he clasps my wrist before I can manage my task.

"I said no."

My throat clogs with emotion, knowing I'll look like a complete fool if he isn't exactly who I suspect him to be.

Call me a fool then, because I force my wrist from his and have him pinned to the wall with the force of my body.

"You don't want to do that," he says softly when I reach for his mask again. "Please don't."

Misplaced despair marks his voice as his brown eyes plead with mine.

It doesn't stop me. Walking out of here, not knowing, is a pain I refuse to suffer through. If he isn't the man I'm desperate to see, I'll apologize and avoid him from now on.

With more gentleness than I feel in my gut, I ease the black fabric down his face until it pools around his throat.

"Impossible," I gasp, stepping away from him.

I touched him. I fucked him a month ago. None of these things are possible with ghosts.

"Max?"

He sighs but doesn't answer. The action tells me he knew it was me long before I could accept the possibility that my childhood friend wasn't actually dead, but alive and well and leaving everyone he loves to think differently. His family was destroyed when I visited them. It was three months after his death that I had enough leave time to go back home, and his father, mother, and sister were all still just existing, unable to move on from the loss.

"How? I went to your grave. I've spent the last ten years griev—"

"Grieving my death?" he spits, acrimony forcing his eyes to squint. His jaw flexes, the hardness something I never remember seeing before.

What an odd time to take note of the new lines that form at the corners of his eyes.

"I died the day you walked away from me."

"How?" I repeat.

"You broke my heart," he seethes.

There's so much anger in his tone, his posture also filled with aggression. Only moments ago, he was on his knees sucking me off, toying with my ass, and taunting me with the same words he said to me the first time he explored me there. He doesn't have the fucking right to be angry with me. Both of our lives could've been so much different from the one we're dealing with right now.

"You faked your death?" My hands begin to tremble, itching to clock him in the jaw. "Who the fuck does that kind of thing? It killed your parents. They've been empty shells for the last ten years. Mia has strug—"

"Don't you say her fucking name!" he roars. "My family isn't your concern. You didn't care enough to stay, so you don't get to pretend you care for them now."

"Didn't care? I fucking care." I draw closer to him, still undecided if I want to wrap my arms around him for a hug or my hands around his throat for hurting everyone the way he did. "I still visit them."

His teeth clench, that hard-cut jaw of his flexing again.

"And when was the last time you set eyes on Ramon and Estella Vazquez? When was the last time you spoke to Mia?"

Shame fills my gut with his words. I haven't reached out to them in over a year, but I know I don't have to make that confession out loud. Somehow, he already knows how long it's been. From the burning look in his eyes, he's kept track of me, more than I've kept over the family that welcomed me like their own when I was younger.

His parents, surprisingly, didn't have an issue when our friendship morphed into more. My dad would've murdered me in anger or as a means to keep the community from discovering that his one and only son wasn't exactly as hetero as he thought.

"This has been fun and all, but I have to get back to Jasmine." He uses his chest to bump me out of the way, and I do my best to ignore the way the brief contact sets my skin on fire. "You need to stay the fuck away from us. The last thing I need is you interfering with what I have going on."

"Jasmine?" My eyes widen at his slip-up, and my hands are shoving him against the wall once again.

When the door inches open, I shove my hand against it and turn the lock. There are a few quick hits on the other side accompanied by several foul words, but then silence fills the room once again.

I focus on his face rather than the implication that the woman we've been playing with is also the niece of my boss. There are probably hundreds of girls with the same name. Nonetheless, his tone and the suggestion that she's a means to an end gets my hackles up.

"What is she to you?" I grab his shoulders, pulling him a couple of inches from the wall before slamming him back again. "You need to explain."

He remains silent.

"Is she a mark?"

Max always teetered on the edge of legal and criminal. Many kids we grew up with did. It comes with growing up poor in a community that's far from thriving. I dabbled in petty theft and breaking into buildings, more for survival than the thrill many of our bored classmates were looking for. Max's family did enough that he didn't have to get involved, but that didn't keep him from being right by my side when the need struck me. Before our senior year, Max had been picked up for several offenses, and the year he was on probation was hell on both of us. His heightened level of supervision didn't keep him from acting out and getting involved with the wrong peer group, no matter how much I begged him to stay out of trouble, if only so we could spend time together.

"You'd be surprised which side of the law I ended up on," he replies, but he doesn't give me anything more.

"You need to explain," I repeat, only this time I grip the front of his throat with one hand.

Even though I have him pinned with my hand tightening around his neck, he doesn't look worried or scared. I'm in the position of authority, yet I can't help but feel like he's the one running the show. Maybe he thinks I wouldn't hurt him. Maybe he believes that what we had in our past is enough to keep me from gripping him tighter.

"She's linked to Cerberus."

My fingers dig into his neck at his confession, and only now do his eyes spark with uncertainty. His confession wipes away the hope I was clinging to that the minx I spanked earlier couldn't be linked to my new life.

"She's just a woman who likes to get fucked," I insist, urging him to let go of whatever it is he's wanting from her.

"She's Jasmine Anderson." His words are released on a ragged breath due to the force I have on his throat.

"You stay the fuck away from her."

I squeeze tighter for a few more seconds before releasing him. I flip the lock on the bathroom door and open it to find a monitor walking toward the restroom, no doubt having been summoned by whoever couldn't get inside earlier.

"We have bathroom scene rooms on the second floor," he says as I storm past. "Go up there if that's your thing. Keep these doors unlocked."

Thankfully, he doesn't grab me to get his point across as I arrow toward where I left the woman sitting on the sofa.

"Of fucking course," I hiss when I find two women tangled around each other in the place she's supposed to be.

A quick look around the club doesn't yield what I hope, and by the time I give up on looking for her and go back to the restroom, Max is also gone.

What a clusterfuck.

Chapter 7

Jasmine

One of the many benefits of growing up around Cerberus are the amenities. Like swimming in the warm waters of Mexico, the temperature of the heated pool washes over my body as I slice through my laps. My apartment complex closes its outdoor pool during the winter months, but even if they didn't, I'd be right here swimming in this one.

I don't have to worry about getting unwelcomed attention from other people who live here, and for the most part, I can swim here without interruption. Landon is the only one underage, and lately, he's discovered girls, so he's more likely to be seen at the mall than here at home where there aren't any prospects.

The splash on the other end of the pool doesn't deter me from making my turn and continuing my laps. My body is languid, even after the orgasms I had yesterday. Toying with the idea of asking King and Carlos to have a little fun outside of the club next time we see each other, I'm startled when my ankle is grabbed just as I kick off the side of the pool to swim in the opposite direction.

Water fills my nose and mouth when I gasp, and I come up sputtering, pool water spraying in every direction.

"What the hell?" I ask, spinning to face the asshole who grabbed me.

Tug, one of the Cerberus guys, doesn't have a grin on his face, and it only pisses me off more.

"We need to talk," he grunts.

"Talk? You could've waited until I was done to ask. You didn't have to nearly drown me."

"I'm not asking." He holds up a towel, his eyes narrowed in my direction while I bob in the water, debating whether or not to even consider speaking with him.

I'm not Tug's friend. Hell, I don't even know his real name. My dad always told me to stay away from the Cerberus guys. He was clear from the time my tits showed up, and some of the guys got caught looking at me that they were off-limits. Yes, many of the guys who worked for my uncle were good looking, but I always obeyed his rules.

The man still standing at the end of the pool glaring at me hasn't started a single conversation since I moved back home from Albuquerque this summer. We've had only the briefest of words with each other when in larger groups around the pool.

Right now, he's staring down at me like he's seen me naked and he isn't exactly pleased with that idea.

Refusing to bend to his command, I swim down to the opposite end of the pool from him and hoist myself out of the water to grab the towel I brought myself.

"What do you want?" I ask as I squeeze the plush towel around my soaked hair.

Cold chills cover every inch of my body as he stalks from his end of the pool to mine.

"We need to talk."

"Yeah, you said that. So, get to talking."

His jaw works, eyes skating from the top of my head to the purple polish on my toes. I don't know if it's his unsolicited attention or the devilish look in his eyes that make my skin tighten, my nipples furl, and my legs go a little weak.

Did his cock just jerk in his jeans?

"Eyes are up here," he snaps.

Steel-gray eyes stare back at me, and the faintest hint of a smirk tugs at the top right corner of his lip before he's frowning again.

"Turn around."

"Excuse me?"

My hands hit my hips with defiance, knowing I'm safe on this property, and even as much as his eyes are eating me up, I know that if he's a Cerberus man, he won't do anything to hurt me.

I cower back a foot when he takes a step closer.

Maybe I was wrong.

"Show me your ass."

"Wh-what?" My eyes dart from him to the door, and I regret immediately coming here to swim. We're enclosed in the indoor pool, and with the way the sun is shining on the glass, I'm fairly certain no one can see us inside.

I may not be as safe as I've allowed myself to believe.

"I'm not going to hurt you." His words are soft, but it's his inability to keep that strong jaw from clenching that won't allow me to trust his words.

"What right do you have to come in here and insist that I let you see my ass?"

"Do you have a butterfly tattoo on your left ass cheek?"

"What the fuck?" I whisper, more to myself than to him.

"You do, don't you?"

I refuse to answer.

"It's blue, pink, and purple." His eyes search mine, and I have no damn clue what he's looking for. "It's much prettier than say a monarch butterfly."

My blood freezes, and it takes a long moment of me staring at him before my heart restarts, and I grow indignant.

"Are you threatening me?"

"No. Far from it."

"Are you planning to blackmail me?"

"Blackmail really isn't my thing."

"Trade your silence for sexual favors?"

As if he can't control himself, his hand reaches for the front of his jeans, but rather than grabbing his junk in some grotesque manner, he simply slides his hand into his pocket.

"Who told you about the club?"

I know this is exactly what he's getting at, and while I wait for him to answer, I chastise myself for ever going in the first place. I knew my fun there was going to be short-lived. There's wasn't a chance my luck would hold out. I just figured I'd end up being replaced or having a lackluster experience with one of the other members there.

"What club?"

"Don't fucking play coy with me."

His eyes continue to roam my body even after I wrap my towel around myself.

"Who told you?"

"I experienced it all for myself, *Lilly*."

My gasp doesn't faze him.

"Kingston Jacks." He holds his palm out in introduction as if I'm dumb enough to place my hand in his.

I only thought I was frozen on the spot. It isn't until my brain decides to piece together everything, and I have to shamefully admit it takes way too long, that the realization hits me square in the chest.

As if struck by an invisible blow, I stumble back a few feet.

"Whoa," he says as he reaches for me, uncaring as he pulls my wet, towel-covered body against his.

If I didn't believe the words coming from his mouth, the familiar scent coming off his clothes would've been all the proof I need.

"King?"

With a gentle grip on my shoulders, he holds me steady before taking a step back.

"Now that the formal introductions are out of the way, we need to talk."

"My dad is going to kill me."

Not only will I have to explain my various kinks to my father, but I'll have to include that I messed around with one of his men. I don't think the simple explanation that I didn't know who he was when we messed around will make any difference. If anything, it'll only make things worse.

I'm contemplating moving out of the country when Tug/Kingston fucking Jacks nudges my shoulder.

"You can freak out later. Right now, we need to talk."

"I fucked one of my dad's men."

"Technically I tongue-fucked and finger-fucked you. My dick hasn't had the pleasure, yet."

Unwelcome arousal hits me with his last word. Did he mean to make it sound like a promise?

He clears his throat, this time not bothering to hide his need for rearranging his thickening erection.

"I need you to tell me everything you know about Ma-Carlos."

"Carlos? What does he have to do with anything? No!" I gasp, covering my mouth with my hand. "Is he another Cerberus member?"

"What?" Tug pulls my hand from my mouth. "Repeat that."

"Is Carlos also Cerberus?"

"Fuck no." He spits the words as if just the idea is blasphemy. "What do you know about him?"

"Other than his dick size? Nothing."

"Jasmine," he warns.

"I don't know anything about him, and I want to keep it that way."

"Have you had any interaction with him outside of the club?"

"No." I take another step back, pissed that he's practically calling me a liar.

"Are you sure?"

"Am I sure? Yes. I haven't had any interactions with a Zorro look-alike in my day-to-day life."

"But you don't know if you've met him unmasked?"

The chills that had dissipated with his nearness and the realization that I've interacted sexually with this man are renewed with his question.

"I don't know." I search his eyes. "Am I in danger?"

"I don't know."

"That's not very reassuring."

"It's the truth. I don't know what he has planned."

"But he does have plans?" His lips turn down, but I refuse to make myself a sitting duck. I'm no longer some little girl who needs her daddy to protect her. I'm a grown woman, and I refuse to be told to stay quiet while the men figure things out. "Tell me."

"I have reason to believe that Carlos sought you out purposefully at the club."

"Like to ask for money so he won't tell my dad I like going there and getting fucked by two guys?"

His eyes widen the same time mine do. I can't believe I just said that out loud.

"I don't think that's his plan."

"Then tell me what it is."

"I don't know."

"Would you tell me if you knew?"

His jaw ticks again. "I think it's best for you to stay at the clubhouse until I can figure out exactly what's going on."

"I'm not a child. I can protect myself."

"Stay at Dominic's if you don't want to stay here."

"I'm more comfortable in my own apartment." I cinch my towel tighter around my middle and walk past him with more bravado than I feel. "I'll be at home if you find anything else out."

"Fucking women," he spits as I leave.

Chapter 8

Tug

I'm not a man who paces.

I'm a man of action.

Yet, I've been wearing a hole in the carpet of my bedroom for the last three hours trying to figure out my next move. I've been over countless scenarios, a multitude of options, and nothing seems like the right plan. It's like playing chess without all the pieces. Without knowing exactly why Max is targeting Jasmine, there's no way for me to counteract whatever his plans are.

Even after consulting with one of my analyst buddies from the Corps, I still have nothing to go on. My non-Cerberus connected friend told me exactly what I was expecting to hear.

"I'm sorry to tell you this, Tug, but your friend died in a car accident ten years ago. Did you want me to dig deeper? Do you think there was foul play?"

"Naw, man. He's just an old friend from high school I was hoping to get in contact with."

"Sorry to be the bearer of bad news."

"Thanks, man." After hanging up, I realize that I handled that call much better than I did the first one.

Ten years ago, it was Mia, Max's twin sister, that reached out to me with the tragic news. She could barely hold her sobs in when she spoke of her brother's death.

My anger only multiplies as I walk back and forth at the foot of my bed.

No matter how long I think about it, I can't figure out why Max would do this to his family. He and Mia both were their parents' absolute joy. Everything that couple did was for the benefit of their children. Is just doesn't make sense for him to destroy them the way he did.

Was he in trouble? Still caught up in the wrong crowd?

Even that doesn't seem plausible. With today's technology, it's all but impossible to fake a death and get away with it. I won't even begin to entertain ideas of government cover-ups and conspiracy theories.

The knock at my door startles me, but I regain my composure in time to pull it open. Scooter stands in the hall with a wide grin on his face.

"What?" I cringe at the anger in my voice. He doesn't deserve my ire.

His head snaps back at my tone. I'm usually the happy-go-lucky kind of guy, known for always being in a good mood. Most of the time, my personality comes off as someone who just goes with the flow. It was a characteristic I developed not long after my dad started kicking my ass. Getting removed from his home, and going into foster care meant no more Max, and that wasn't an option.

"Bad time?" he asks, looking over my shoulder to peer into my room like whatever was behind me would explain my attitude.

"No. Just tired." I rub my hand over my eyes for emphasis even though I'm wired like a fucking bomb.

"Some of the guys are heading out to *Jake's* after we're briefed. Gonna go have some fun before we head out tomorrow evening."

"Tomorrow evening? I didn't get the message. Where are we going?"

"South America," he answers.

"Fuck." We've spent more time in Caracas and Bogota these days than we do in New Mexico.

"Seems we didn't cut the head off the snake last time as we thought. Another three girls have gone missing. The community is in an uproar because a local girl was one of them this time."

I don't bother mentioning that even if we did eradicate one trafficking group that another one just pops up in its place before the wheels go up on the plane as we fly out of the country.

"They weren't very quick to help us when it was only tourists," I complain.

"I think this trip will take longer than the last time."

"Great."

"So, do you want to tag along to *Jake's*?"

"Not this time. When is the briefing?"

Scooter looks down at his watch. "In fifteen minutes."

"See you there."

I close the door before he can answer, not quite ready to face the other members of my team. After splashing water on my face, I lift my head and stare at myself in the mirror, wondering if I look the same and different to Max like he did to me. I can understand him being bitter about me leaving but questioning my grief after hearing of his death was taking things too far.

I need to somehow infiltrate the guest manifest from *Hale-ish* so I can figure out what credentials Carlos/Max used to get into the club. Nothing illegal goes on there as far as I know, but it's pretty fucking exclusive. The only reason I got in is because Garrett Hale offers free VIP memberships to all of Cerberus. Call it a perk of the job if one is so inclined. Getting that information may be hard to come by. I expect that information to be closely guarded, just like the info Cerberus has. The encryption would be a bitch to get through, and even then, probably nearly impossible to grab without being noticed.

I'm mulling over my options again as I walk into the meeting room located in the center of the Cerberus clubhouse. As the last one to arrive, Kincaid looks up at me before letting his eyes fall down to the open folder on the table.

"Xavier Cortez's crew wasn't the primary," he begins as I take my seat. "His older brother, Luis Cortez, will be your focus this time around."

"Is he the head of the snake?" Scooter asks.

"We won't be sure until his compound is breached, and we're able to get a better look at things," Shadow answers. He clicks a button on the remote, and the flat screen on the wall behind him comes to life.

"We saw that building the last time we were there," Rocker hisses. "A local told us it was owned by some American billionaire."

"They didn't lie," Shadow confirms as he switches the map for a photo of a very El Chapo looking guy. "Luis Cortez is technically American, first generation born in El Paso. He preferred his parents' homeland to Texas."

"What's with the seventies haircut and sideburns?" Grinch asks right before sneezing into the crook of his elbow. "Is this an old picture?"

"Bless you," several guys say.

"Only about six months old," Kid says with a sigh. "He's known for emulating Joaquín Guzmán. He gives to the community for protecting him."

"Nothing like saying 'thanks' with money paid to fuck children," I mutter.

Kincaid ignores me, but I don't miss the frown on his lips.

"How does Sinaloa feel about this?" one of the other guys asks, no doubt an attempt to get us back on track.

"They're not happy," Shadow answers, flipping the screen to another shot. This one, the graphic aftermath of a bloody battle should make me cringe, but the things I've seen in person have hardened me to having outward emotions like that. Internally, I'm a raging fire, ready to bring hell down on anyone and everyone even remotely connected to these fuckers.

"This is from four months ago. This isn't the first or the last time, the Sinaloa and Cortez Cartels have had disagreements. You'll need to be extra vigilant when doing recon. We're looking for Luis, but so are many others."

I refuse to meet Dominic's eyes when he speaks. The man is like a walking lie detector, and I'm sure just one look at me, and he'll be able to decipher exactly what I've done with his precious daughter.

"The community is in an uproar because one of Cortez's men snatched a local girl from in front of her school," Kid continues. "Her father had been killed just a few hours before for refusing to allow some of Cortez's men into his shop before he was scheduled to open. She's eleven. The other two who were taken the same day are a couple of friends that were there on mission work."

The screen comes alive with the smiling faces of three females, one a cute little girl whose front teeth are still a little too big for her face. The other two are driver's license pictures, one of a honey-haired girl, the other of a woman of Hispanic descent.

"The church reached out to us for Maria Yves and Caroline Spring." Shadow uses the laser to point to each of the women. "It was after speaking with the minister that we discovered the abduction of the younger girl."

"The dossiers in front of you will tell you everything you need to know," Kincaid adds.

"This says there's only enough space for a five-man crew." Scooter's eyes shoot up to our president. "That means a couple of guys will have to stay behind?"

"I'm taking volunteers," Kincaid says, already preparing himself for a battle.

Several guys grumble, crossing their arms over their chests and leaning back. He'll be forced to pick if no one volunteers.

"I'll stay behind." I raise my hand as Shadow's eyebrows raise. "Got some shit I need to take care of this week, anyway."

"I think I'm getting the flu," Grinch says.

Jokingly, the guys on either side of him inch away blatantly. The first time I saw something like that happen, joking while talking about something so serious, I thought people were apathetic, and it pissed me off. After breaching a couple of these trafficking spots and seeing the horrific things these people have experienced, I realized joking takes the edge off. Without it, we'd be empty inside. The things we see and have to do sometimes would eat us alive.

"I need two more," Kincaid prompts.

Begrudgingly, two other guys raise their hands.

"Great. Wheels up tomorrow evening at eighteen hundred hours," Kincaid says. "Play this right guys, and you should be home for Christmas."

"Keep your heads down," Dominic adds. "Per usual, these guys shoot first. They don't even bother with questions after."

The room begins to clear, and I follow along with the other guys, heading to my room before I can be asked again about going to *Jake's*. There's only one place I'm going tonight. Thankfully, I'm a weirdo who doesn't mind a little surveillance work.

Chapter 9

Jasmine

I told him I'd be fine, that I could take care of myself.

I'm a damn liar.

It's like the one time I binged on *Supernatural* for two days straight. Once again, I'm seeing shadows and hearing noises that before the little confrontation at the pool earlier wouldn't even register. I couldn't even bring myself to get in the shower to wash the chlorine from my hair because I waited until after it got dark outside to even consider needing one.

A thump on the other side of the wall has me tucking my feet closer to my body. My handgun sits on the coffee table a mere two feet away. I'm not holding it because I'm so jumpy, I'm certain I'd shoot myself if I startle again.

Music wafts through the walls, which is saying a lot since I live in a really nice complex. It was the only one my dad would allow, as it's the safest one in town. Normally, I'd dig my feet in and tell the overprotective man that I'd live wherever I want, but as it turns out, safety is really important to me, increasingly so the older I get. My blinders aren't on like they were when I was a kid. There's no one in my daily life that keeps me from watching the news, and after a car wreck with a friend my sophomore year in college, I now know I'm not invincible.

I rub at my side, certain I can feel the ghost pain from those broken ribs.

"I'm losing my damn mind," I mutter, giving the remote control another look.

I'm terrified out of my damn mind, but I'm also bored. The terror wins out because I refuse to turn on the TV in fear that I won't hear someone if they're coming to get me.

Something thuds against my front door, and I'm unable to keep the shriek from escaping my lips. Someone laughs on the other side. I should run to my room, but it's the taunting giggle on the other side of my door that makes my spine stiffen. Grabbing the Springfield from the coffee table, I make my way across the room until my eye is plastered to the peephole.

The young couple from next door that moved in just a couple weeks ago is making out in the hallway like a couple of teenagers. Relief washes over me at the sight, and I once again feel ridiculous.

Not enough to go climb in my bed to go to sleep but enough to get back on the couch, waiting and listening for the next noise to scare the shit out of me.

Who could Carlos be?

I don't know much about what my dad and Cerberus do, not the details at least. I know they help people, rescue abducted persons. Is it possible Carlos is getting intel in order to abduct me?

Just the thought makes my skin crawl, and I finally realize I'm not safe here. Even though I'll have to make up some lie to my dad, I know I'll be safe there. I refuse to admit my fear to Tug, so the clubhouse isn't an option.

Springing up from the couch, I head to my room and pack a bag.

"I'll tell him I saw a bug," I say out loud to myself like a truly insane person. "I can get a couple of days at his house while arrangements are made for fumigation."

Happy with my plan, I grab my handgun from the coffee table and tuck it into the waistband of my yoga pants. It's not the safest way to carry it, but I don't want to stay here long enough to go back to my room and grab my holster. After shouldering my packed duffel, I look out the peephole one last time, grateful the horny couple have managed to get inside of their own apartment.

My foot taps as I keep an eye on the hallway while waiting for the elevator. I refuse to use the stairwell. I've seen what happens to women in those things. Primetime TV taught me to avoid them while I'm alone.

"Come on," I hiss, hitting the down button about ten times in a row.

Relief washes over me when the doors open with a ding, only to fade when the doors close me inside. *What if someone gets on with me? Will I have the courage or even the ability to defend myself? I'm a good shot, but what if I don't even have time to get to my gun?*

My shirt is lifted, hand on the butt of my gun when the elevator opens.

"What the fuck?" Tug hisses while I scream at the sight of him. "What are you planning on doing with that thing?"

His hand is on my wrist, angling the gun away and at the ground before I even know what's happening.

"Please don't hurt me," I whisper.

"Hurt you?"

I relinquish the gun, my eyes filling with tears when I watch him tuck it into his jeans at his back.

"Come on."

It isn't until he lightly grips me at my elbow that I realize he's not only stepped inside of the elevator with me, but we're back on my floor.

"Where were you going?" he asks as he digs into my front pocket and pulls my keys out. A second later, he's opening my apartment door and is guiding me inside.

"To my dad's," I answer without much thought. "I saw a bug."

"Bullshit. You've been cowering in this damn living room for the last three hours. You didn't see a bug. You're terrified."

"H-how would you know that?"

He points across the room to my front window. It's the only bad thing about the corner apartment. Although I have two hundred square feet more on the inside; it also faces the street.

"I was in my car."

"And you can see through walls?"

"Infrared," he mutters.

"Well, that's not intrusive at all, now is it?" Sarcasm is much better than the sheer terror I felt only moments ago.

"Do you still want to go to your parents' house?" he asks. "I can drive you over there."

"I want my gun back," I mutter.

"You're safer without it. Do you want to go to your parents'?"

"I'm a licensed holder."

"You're more likely to shoot yourself before being able to defend yourself."

I remain silent, refusing to acknowledge that I was recently thinking about the exact same thing.

"Last time, do you want me to take you to your parents' house?"

"And how would you explain being there? Or is that your plan? Get us together so you can reveal my deviant desires? He'd kill you for touching me."

"Your desires aren't deviant. Also, I have no plans to tell your father what we've done, but if you're too scared to stay here, then I'll do what needs to be done to make you feel safe, even if that means facing your father's wrath."

"Willing to die?"

He sighs, both of his strong hands rubbing down his face. "Your dad won't kill me for the things we've done."

"You put a lot of faith in a man you hardly know anything about," I return.

"If nothing else, the man isn't rash. I didn't force you into anything, and even though he may not be happy with it, he certainly wouldn't be murderous. Now, if you don't want to go there, I can take you to the clubhouse."

"That's not any better," I remind him.

"Fine."

He takes the strap of my bag off my arm and disappears down the hallway.

"What are you doing?" I snap when I follow him only to find him pulling my clothes from the bag.

"If you won't leave, then I'll stay here with you."

"Fat damn chance."

"You want to stay alone?" His gray eyes turn to me in challenge as he holds up a pair of lacy white panties.

"I can drive myself." When I reach to snap the underwear from his hand, he pulls it back before my fingers can brush the fabric.

"Any chance of convincing you to stay here? I'd love to see how these look with that sexy tattoo of yours."

I bite my lip, knowing he grows hot at the sight. I am my father's daughter, and he taught me from an early age to observe everything going on around me. He was sure to let me know that most people's actions can be read seconds before they even decide to make them. It's in their eyes, the twitch of their fingers or the way they move their body to prepare.

Both nights at *Hale-ish*, Tug's eyes grew darker each time he saw my teeth digging into my own flesh. I imagined him thinking about what my mouth could do to him. He's looking at me exactly the same way now.

"I think you staying is an amazing idea," I purr as I slide up against his body.

I'm playing with fire, but the thought of staying here alone isn't something I'll think about. Going to my parents' house is no longer appealing either.

Chapter 10

Tug

"This isn't what I had in mind," I mutter as Jasmine tries to shove a stack of sheets and a pillow in my hands.

"The couch is actually really comfortable." She grins at me, but I see no humor in the situation right now. "Can I have my gun back?"

"Not a fucking chance," I answer. "The last thing I want is to get shot if I have to get up to piss."

"You could leave, you know. You invited yourself to stay."

"And you said it was a wonderful idea," I grumble as I shake out a sheet and begin to cover the plush leather sofa with it.

"Sorry if you thought I meant something different than offering the couch."

Her voice is playful, and fuck if she doesn't have those teeth digging into her lip again when I reach for the second sheet.

"You know, there's an awful lot of room in that king-sized bed of yours."

"Are you trying to get into my panties?"

"Trying to get you out of them is more like it." Her eyes follow my tongue when I lick at my bottom lip like I want to lick at the pretty pink cunt of hers.

"I-I don't think that's a good idea." Her throat works on a swallow, but her eyes never leave my mouth.

"You can put on your mask if it makes you feel more comfortable," I offer.

"Don't be a dick."

"That's not my intention at all. I can't think of a better way to make you feel safe than making you come."

"I have work in less than five hours. Sleep—" I raise my eyebrows at her words, "—actually sleeping is the only thing on my mind right now."

"I bet if I dipped my fingers inside your yoga pants, your pussy couldn't lie to me."

She doesn't give in as I hope; rather, she shoves the pillow still in her hands against my chest. "We may have fooled around at the club, but I'm not interested in you that way any longer now that I know who you are."

"Shame," I say before tossing the pillow on the couch before reaching my arms out to her. "Hug good night?"

"Nope."

She turns on her heels and walks away. A second later, her bedroom door slams closed, but it's the sound of the lock engaging that makes me go from semi to rock solid. It doesn't take ten minutes of me lying on the couch with my eyes focused on the ceiling before I hear a buzzing noise.

I'm off the couch and standing at her bedroom door in the next breath. Needed sleep my ass. She's just as turned on as I am, and even though I'd never force a woman, that doesn't keep me from wanting to kick her door down and spank that tight ass of hers.

My knuckles hit the door twice, and I grin at her gasp.

"What are you doing in there?" Accusation laces my tone, and I know she knows I just busted her masturbating.

"N-nothing. Go get back on the couch or leave."

"Sure you don't want some help in there?"

Silence surrounds us as she debates whether to let me in or not.

"I've got things under control." The buzzing starts again.

The sound is electrifying, but it's the whimpers that accompany it that has me reaching for my dick. If I haven't heard them before at the club, I'd wonder if the sounds she's making were all for show, but when we were together, those same throaty moans left her lips then, too.

"There's no sense in both of us masturbating when we could spend the next hour pleasing each other."

All that can be heard is the damn toy she insists on using, and it makes me visualize her teeth biting at that plump bottom lip of hers.

"I could lick that sweet pussy of yours," I bargain as I lower my zipper and grip my aching cock. "Maybe slide inside of you for the first time."

Another whimper.

"Your cunt was so tight on my fingers. I've fantasized for weeks about how it would wrap around my dick."

"Please," she pants. "More."

I'm torn between using my words to get her off and walking away, refusing to give her what she's begging for.

I must be a sadist because the words are what I opt for. Closing my eyes and pulling the sight of her naked and filled with pleasure from my memory, I continue.

"My mouth is watering to taste you again, but only after I spank your ass for making me so hard it hurts. Fuck that feels good," I grunt stroking down my dick, wishing she was on her knees at my feet taking me in her mouth instead.

"Kingston," she moans.

"Open the door, Jasmine. Let me see you come."

"Oh, God," she hisses before releasing a long husky moan.

"Goddammit," I hiss, pinching the end of my cock, so I don't spray her bedroom door with cum.

The release only leaves me wanting more. It was hot, don't get me wrong, but knowing there was something much more exciting on the other side of that door is enough to piss me off. After cleaning up in the bathroom, I huff like a child and throw myself on her couch. I'm still awake three hours later when she shuffles to the kitchen to make a pot of coffee.

I feel her eyes turn to me before she disappears into the other room, but I pretend to be asleep, wanting the element of surprise.

When the water runs in the sink, I climb off the couch and make my way silently into the kitchen. For someone so jumpy last night, she doesn't seem to be wrapped in fear this morning.

"Make enough for both of us," I say, right against her back.

Her scream makes me chuckle, but when she turns bloodshot eyes on me in a glare, I back away a couple of feet.

"Not a morning person I take it?" I hold my hands up in surrender, but from the narrowing of her eyes, I can tell she knows that I'm not ceding a damn thing.

"I only got like two hours of sleep," she mutters before pouring water into the coffee pot.

"Could've gotten two and a half if you hadn't gotten your toy out," I remind her.

She's not facing me, but the messy knot of hair on her head allows me to watch the tips of her ears burn with embarrassment. The sight is odd considering the way she rocked her hips on my mouth without shame the first time we hooked up at the club. Maybe the mask does provide her an extreme level of anonymity.

"Then again," I continue when she doesn't speak, "orgasms usually help people sleep more soundly."

"Can we not discuss what happened last night?" She busies herself with the filter and coffee at a speed so slow it makes me wonder if this is actually part of her routine or if she only uses caffeine on rough mornings.

I'm grinning at her when she finally turns around to face me.

"What about the things that happened at the club?" I smile wider. "Are those off-limits, too?"

"All of it is off-limits."

"So, you aren't open to the idea of getting off before work? I hear morning sex really gets you revved for the day." I lower my voice as I inch closer to her. "It really gets the juices flowing, at least it does in my experience."

"We don't have time for sex."

Not the rejection I was anticipating. I was already turned on before she left her room. Just thinking of her sounds the last couple of hours have left me aroused, but right now, I can't think of anything better to do with my time than sink inside of her.

"So just you then?"

My hands find her hips, and much to my surprise, she doesn't back away. Not that she has much room to move since I've all but caged her against the countertop.

"J-just me?" she stammers.

"Just you," I repeat, my lips finding the delicate skin between her neck and her ear. "Do you wanna come before dealing with idiotic college students?"

If she's surprised that I know where she works, she doesn't show it.

"Hmm?" I prod when she doesn't answer me. I nip at her neck as my fingers dig in harder to her hips. "What do you say? I can be quick."

"Wh-what about you?"

"I'll have the taste of your pussy on my mouth all day while I jack off in your bed waiting for you to get home."

"Mmm," she moans, and I don't know if it's the thought of me defiling her sacred place or the things my mouth is doing to her neck.

She hasn't rejected me, so I test my luck by sliding my fingers past the waistband of her yoga pants to grip her ass.

"And when you get home, I'm going to fuck this ass of yours." She moans again. "I remember you saying you liked that."

"Kingston," she moans when I let my hands fall lower until fingers from both hands are prodding at her slick entrance.

"What do you say?"

"Please," she answers.

It only takes the blink of an eye to push down her bottoms and lift her to sit on the counter. In the next breath, her legs are over my shoulders, and my mouth is on her hot cunt.

"Oh, God." Her fingers tangle in my hair as my tongue travels over her flesh. "So good. Don't stop."

A masked gunman knocking down her door, hell, her father showing up right now wouldn't be enough to make me pull my mouth from her.

I drink her down, lapping at her, swirling my tongue until she begins to tremble. She's close, and as much as I want to draw this out, I also know she has to go to work. There will be time for taking things slower later. Right now, she needs to come. With a nip to her hard clit, she does, spectacularly so. It takes strength I wasn't planning to use just to keep her ass on the counter as her body convulses against my mouth. When she's pulling on my hair, urging me to stop, I lick her hard again, not stopping a moment before I'm good and ready.

"Coffee's made," I tell her as I pull my mouth away.

I lick her taste from my lips, and she's staring at my mouth like she wants to do it for me, but I can't allow that to happen. My lips on hers would mean more than it should, and I'm here to protect her from whatever shit Max is cooking up, not make the woman fall for me. Call it egotistical, but women are emotional creatures, toss in great sex, orgasms so strong you grow weak in the knees, and it's a recipe for disaster.

Chapter 11

Jasmine

"You really are planning to stay here all day?" I ask as Kingston kicks off his jeans before heading to my room.

"I can leave if you want." He leaves me to make the decision, glancing from my bed and back to me twice.

If he leaves, he may not come back, and as much as getting involved with him means trouble, I can't seem to resist. I go to clubs for great sex, never having found it outside of the walls of such places, but now the great sex is here. Well, what I can imagine will be great sex, since we've never actually fucked yet. Him being here, clearly as willing to fuck as I am, just means I can skip the eight-hour drive to Denver. I don't want him to leave.

"Don't come on my sheets," I warn as I pull my top over my head and turn toward my closet.

"Show me your tits."

I go to toss him a seductive, teasing smile over my shoulder, but he's the one seducing me. Already having climbed into my bed, I watch his hand move over his cock under my sheet. The black boxer briefs he was wearing only moments ago have been cast to the floor. He's a stealthy guy, that's for sure.

"I have to go to work."

"And I can appreciate that but turn to face me while you get dressed. That way I can think of all the ways I'm going to *un*dress you when you get back."

I roll my eyes but do as he says. His lips parts when I pull on the lace panties he got his hands on last night, but his breath hitches when I snap the matching bra into place.

"That thing barely holds those gorgeous tits of yours." I smile, reaching for my blouse next. His eyes are laser-focused on my disappearing skin, and by the time I bend down to pull the pencil skirt up my thighs, his hand is working overtime. "That fucking skirt."

"You like it?"

"Come here."

Without bothering to zip my skirt, I cross the room and stand beside the bed.

"Finish me off."

He tosses the sheet back, revealing his straining erection.

"Jesus," I say at the sight of him.

He's veiny and thick, and if I let myself think about it long enough, I may chicken out on what he offered for this evening.

"Jasmine," he moans, and my name in that tone moves me into action.

My lips wrap around him, my teeth barely past his crown when he explodes in my mouth. I swallow as much as I can, but the flood is almost too much. What I don't swallow on the first try, I lick away on the second.

"Dammit," he hisses when I clean him up with more suction than necessary. "That mouth of yours."

"Zip me up," I tell him as I turn my back and tuck in my blouse.

He obliges, his fingers taking longer than he needs to get the zipper up.

For good measure, he swats my ass before I can walk across the room to grab my heels.

"Are you really staying here all day?" I ask as I lean one hand on the dresser and tug on my left shoe before doing the same with the right.

"Not all day. I'll probably get a couple of hours of sleep, and then I got shit I have to start working on."

"Carlos?" I ask.

"Yeah," he answers, but he refuses to meet my eyes.

"How do you know him?"

"I don't know Carlos." His jaw starts clenching the way it did at the pool yesterday, so I know I'm not going to get anything out of him.

"Will you tell me if I'm in danger?"

"Of course."

"Am I in danger now?"

"I don't know the answer to that. For the immediate future, park close to entrances and keep an eye out for danger. I don't think anything will happen in broad daylight but keep your eyes open." He holds his hand out. "Give me your phone, so I can put in my number. Call me if you see anything suspicious."

I dig in my purse on the dresser and produce my phone after entering the unlock code. After he enters his information, I hear his phone chime in the living room.

"Will you be here when I get back?"

"Do you want me to be here when you get back?"

I shrug. I'm not trying to be coy, but I'm also not going to beg the man to stay.

"What time will you get home?"

"I'll be at the clubhouse by two and usually finish my laps by three-thirty. That puts me back here no later than four-fifteen."

"Why don't you just stay with me at the clubhouse?"

"There's no privacy there. Everyone knows everyone's business. I'm not dealing with that on top of whatever is going on with Carlos."

"The guys are leaving this evening."

"My dad and uncle will still be around. I'm not ready for that conversation."

"Understood."

"I only got scared last night when the sun went down," I confide. "I'm sure I won't be scared at all tonight, so if you have something else going on, I don't require a babysitter."

I straighten my spine, needing to say the words even though I hope he's here later.

"Have a good day at work," he says, but he doesn't tell me one way or the other about his evening plans. It'll leave me on edge all damn day.

"Bye, dear," I tell him playfully.

His laughter follows me out of the apartment.

***

Some days teaching college is an ass-whipping by itself. Today, after hardly any sleep last night, and a Monday on top of that, my day is destined to be one of my worst.

Dealing with whiny freshman and sophomores who think they know it all tests my patience until I'm able to hide out in my car for the hour and a half I'm given for lunch between classes. Sitting out in the open probably isn't the best idea, but even the threat of someone grabbing me or trying to hurt me doesn't deter me. I even manage a forty-five-minute nap before waking up not knowing what year it is and in an even fouler mood than before I fell asleep.

The students must have sensed my mood before class even started because even Wesley didn't try his luck today.

By one-thirty, I'm climbing in my car and mentally listing all the reasons why just going home to crash is the best idea ever, but twenty minutes later I'm parking in front of the clubhouse, knowing that using energy on swimming will ensure a restful night.

I struggle into my wet bathing suit from yesterday, having forgotten to even get my bag out of my car in my rush to get inside where I thought I'd feel safer.

"Gross," I mutter, situating the straps on my shoulders before walking out of the changing room to dive into the pool.

"Hey, sweetheart."

I gasp when my father speaks, but it's not his voice or the sight of him sitting in a lounge chair beside my mom that shocks me. It's the sight of Tug as he holds up his beer in a mock salute that is out of place.

"Hey, Daddy." I wave at him, knowing he can tell I'm guilty of something before telling my mom hi.

"How many laps are you going to swim today?" My mom doesn't really like the water, claiming that it ruins her hair, but I can't seem to get enough.

"I don't know. I usually swim until I'm tired."

"You look tired already," Mom says as she stands before coming toward me to angle my chin up, so she can look into my eyes. "Did you stay up all night grading papers?"

"One of the downfalls of being a teacher," I lie.

"You need to make sure you get plenty of rest," Dad says, as he too stands, wrapping an arm around my mother as he joins us.

"I'll sleep better tonight."

"Everyone is getting together here on Saturday for a meal," Dad says as he presses a kiss to my temple. "Plan on being here."

"Yes, sir," I tell him, grateful when they walk out the door.

The sound of Kingston's beer bottle lowering on the glass tabletop beside the loungers makes me round on him.

"What are you doing here?" I seethe. "Trying to start shit in front of my parents?"

His head snaps back. "I live here, Jasmine."

"Still," I hiss. "Beers with my dad? Really? What are you doing?"

"I was already out here when they joined me," he clarifies. "They've only been here for a few minutes. I think they were going to get a little freaky. They were quite disappointed to see me sitting here."

"Why are you in here?"

"Waiting for you, of course."

"I'm just here to get my laps in." I drop my towel on the lounger on the opposite side from his. "And don't talk about my parents and sex in the same sentence. It's gross."

"I bet you mom is a fre—"

"Say another word, and I'll kill you."

He laughs, so I make sure to splash him when I jump in the pool.

Chapter 12

Tug

I don't know if it was the sight of seeing me poolside with her parents or what, but it's been almost two weeks since I had the taste of her on my lips. Two weeks filled with the torture of being so close while sleeping on her couch and not touching her.

Even though I'd been invited to their family dinner, I turned it down, opting to hang out at *Jake's* with the other guys that didn't go to South America. Not having the opportunity to touch her didn't mean I didn't keep my eyes on her every chance I got, so attending a dinner where others would be able to watch me watching her wasn't an option.

It didn't, however, keep me from being at her place once the meal was over.

Even now, a week later, and she still won't give me any hints that she wants me. The first week, I poked and prodded, made every word from my mouth an innuendo, suggested getting naked every chance I got. The second week we've just kind of co-existed. Other than her asking me each morning before she left for work if I was going to be back again in the evening, she hasn't made any outward indication that she wants me here. She isn't rude. She isn't making comments about taking over part of her space, but she isn't throwing herself at me either. My cock has been hard for her for weeks, and she doesn't seem even the slightest bit concerned or interested in doing anything about it.

Nothing else has come up about Max, and since she hasn't asked, I haven't said anything. Fact is, I don't have anything new to share. I've found it's impossible to get information on a ghost.

"Where are you going?"

Her tone isn't accusatory, but I don't fight my smile when she watches me tug up my jeans. Her eyes are focused on the front of my boxers and stay there until my jeans are zipped.

"It's masquerade night at the club."

"And?" Her eyes finally lift to mine, wary and full of unease. "You're going?"

"Of course, I am. I'll bet my life that Carlos will be back tonight. We need to have a little chat."

"I'm going with you." She turns from me and heads toward her bedroom.

"Not going to happen," I tell her after following her down the hall.

"You can't stop me." She's deep in her closet, but her words are as clear as day.

"You're not going," I reiterate when she walks out carrying less fabric than would make a decent outfit.

"I don't answer to you," she huffs before pulling her top over her head.

I open my mouth to threaten to tie her to a chair, gagged, but then she reaches for the hem of her shirt, and suddenly, I'm struck mute. Even though she hasn't been coming on to me or letting me seduce her, she hasn't regained whatever modesty she had prior to my first day here, and she didn't have much then.

Her bra is tossed to the side next, and I stare, entranced at the sight of her heavy breasts. My mouth literally waters with the need to feel her dark nipples on my tongue. I'd like to think it's my eyes on her that tightens her nipples, but it's probably the apartment's cool air.

"We could just stay here," I offer. There's nothing like the sight of a half-naked woman to make a man forget what his plans were to begin with.

"And how would that afford you the opportunity to speak with Carlos?"

Too soon, her breasts are covered by the fabric of a slinky red top, the outline of her hard nipples pressing against the satin.

"No bra?"

Her shoulder hitches as she reaches for a short skirt. "I don't see the point in one."

"You can't go." My throat is dry, my cock hard as steel.

"If he wants to speak to me, then me being there will get that the fastest."

"I'm not using you as bait for a man whom I have no clue of his intentions."

"You won't get far without me."

Shiny black stilettos adorn her feet next, and I'm close to suggesting we stay here again. Max hasn't made so much as a peep the last two weeks, so there's a good chance he took my warning and changed his mind about whatever he had been planning for Jasmine.

"So, what? You plan on going in there and playing detective?"

"I don't really have a plan."

"You look like you plan to play in that getup."

"That's what the club's for, right?"

The vixen winks at me before sitting down at her vanity to begin applying her makeup.

"You really think he'll approach us if he sees us messing around?"

My cock is willing to take the chance.

She huffs, and I pull my eyes from the smooth skin of her neck to meet hers in the mirror.

"What?"

"Only a fool would think that would work."

My eyes narrow. "You want me to send you there alone?"

That same shoulder raises again. "Bait doesn't have a bodyguard."

"No fucking way." I take a step back, distancing myself from her suggestion. "What if you're approached by someone else?"

She sets down some sort of makeup brush before looking over her shoulder at me. "Then I guess I'll just have to play my part until Carlos gets there."

Her teeth dig into her bottom lip when I growl. Just the idea of her letting someone else touch her, taste her skin, when she's been ambivalent to me for the last two weeks makes me see red.

"Besides, it's been weeks since I've had a really good orgasm. I'm due."

My jaw aches from how hard I'm clenching my teeth. "I've been offering to fuck you into a coma for the last two weeks."

The reminder doesn't seem to faze her.

"I like to fuck at the club."

"Hurry up then. We can get there early and fuck like rabbits."

Her airy chuckle does nothing to dispel my need for her.

"You don't seem too keen on the idea," I point out when she continues to apply her makeup. "Did I do something wrong?"

"What do you mean?" Her question is a little warped with how she's holding her mouth to apply lipstick.

"One minute you're coming on my tongue and letting me nut in your mouth with the promise of fucking your ass, and then later that day, you're doing nothing but giving me the cold shoulder."

Her eyes fall to the items strewn across her vanity. I wait her out, feeling one hundred percent like a loser for even being concerned. Voicing my issue with the last two weeks was something I've debated over and over while trying to fall asleep on her damn couch the last two weeks. Guilt swims in my gut for even letting the words fall from my lips. She has every right to deny me, as any person does when they don't want to have sex. She doesn't have to fall to her knees to suck my cock or bend over and let me fuck her just because the mood strikes me, but it's more of the rejection than missing out on the actual act that has been bothering me.

"I had a chance to think about things."

"And you realized you didn't want to fuck me?"

Pressing the issue seems like a bad plan, but I've already opened the door, might as well walk through it.

"My wanting to fuck you isn't the issue. It's been hell being so close to you and not being able to touch you."

"Not being able? Is your pussy broken."

Her lip twitches with mirth when she turns on her vanity stool to face me. "My pussy is fine."

"I wouldn't know," I mumble, taking another step back and sitting on the end of her bed.

"Getting involved with you is a bad idea."

"Does this have anything to do with your parents being at the pool that day?"

"Part of it," she confesses. "My main issue has more to do with what happens after you figure out what's going on with Carlos."

"What happens then?"

She shrugs. "Who knows?"

"And *that's* the problem? The unknown?"

"Aren't you concerned about it? What will happen, how you'll feel after it's all over?"

"I haven't given it much thought."

"Such a typical man," she grumbles as she stands from the vanity and walks out of the room.

I shoot off the bed to follow her. "What's that supposed to mean?"

"You're thinking with your dick."

"I use my brain sometimes, too."

"Then use your brain to try to figure out what your plans are with Carlos. You have over seven hours to work it out on the way to Denver."

She's heading out the door, uncaring if I'm behind her, so I rush to shove my boots on my feet and grab my gun, wallet, and cell phone off the coffee table before running after her.

"What's wrong?" I ask when I catch up and find her standing near the covered parking.

"I usually take my bike."

Looking over, I see the same motorcycle I questioned weeks ago sitting in the spot marked with her apartment number. Omen or not, I'm glad I went back into the club that night. If I hadn't, Carlos could've made a move on her in the club, and I wouldn't have had a clue.

"I brought one of the SUVs from the clubhouse."

I point to the black vehicle in the visitor's parking.

"That thing only gets like fifteen miles to the gallon. We can take my car."

She points to a Kia Soul, and I don't bother to hide the chuckle that comes from my mouth.

"I need more room than that box allows." I cross the lot and open the passenger door. "Get in so we can get this night over with."

As I close the door on her huffing, I don't bother to tell her that I'll need every inch of the room the SUV allows because if Carlos shows up tonight, he's leaving with us.

Chapter 13

Jasmine

In case Carlos is already here, Tug and I entered the club separately.

He went in first with strict instructions on my options of where he would allow me to sit so he could keep an eye on me. Not that it's any different from the last two weeks. His eyes have been glued to some part of me since he showed up at my apartment and never left.

"Are you sure?" the guy behind the counter asks as he reaches for the single band. "Seems like a big jump from just green and purple."

"I'm feeling a little wild tonight," I respond, holding my wrist out so he can attach the black band.

I smile politely, nodding my head periodically as he goes into his long spiel about consent and how the band doesn't give anyone who wants to touch me actual permission. When he's done, I thank him and enter the common area of the club.

The music is low and sultry, the room sparse with people with it being so early in the evening.

With trembling fingers, I readjust the mask over my eyes. For all the bravado I showed back at my apartment, anxiety is hitting me hard now that I'm here.

Dylan laughs, looking a little unsure when I order two glasses of whiskey. His eyes dart from my eyes to my black band, but eventually, he obliges and fixes my drinks.

"Went ahead and put both in one glass," he says as he slides the tumbler across the bar. "Hope you don't mind."

"Not a problem," I tell him with a saccharine-sweet smile. I should make him repour them because it's clear that he didn't give me the allotted amount, but I'm sure it has more to do with a concern of the trouble I can get into in here than them wanting to save on alcohol costs.

What is it about men making decisions about women for their own good? Even in a sex club where damn near anything is allowed and celebrated, machismo is thick and ever-present.

Keeping my eyes on him, I tilt the drink and down the entire glass. It takes everything I have not to gag and squeeze my eyes closed when the strong liquid hits my gut. I must manage to maintain the hard look I'm giving him because he only chuckles again before walking away to help another customer.

With my liquid courage burning a hole in my empty stomach, I grab a bottle of water from the glass front refrigerator and make my way to one of the approved locations Kingston and I discussed on the way here.

To the right of the sofa I settle on, several men are talking and lounging, seemingly without a care in the world, none of them Carlos. To my left, a man looks around the room anxiously as if maybe this is his first time here. The woman connected to his hip watches two men play on the St. Andrew's cross on the other side of the room with lust-filled eyes. When her partner follows her gaze, it's clear he's thinking they made a mistake by coming here.

Uncapping my bottle of water and lifting it to my lips, I watch her lean in and whisper something to the man. His head snaps back before it begins shaking violently as he refuses whatever her offer was.

"I bet he makes her leave before she even gets the chance to play."

I turn my head expecting to see a man standing alone. My smile widens when I see not only a man but two gorgeous women on either side of him, one tall and blonde, the other a small-framed woman with dark brown hair.

"Mind if we join you?" the blonde on his right asks, her smile revealing perfect white teeth encircled by plump lips.

Kingston would love her mouth, I think as I nod and spread my arms wide in agreement to her question. "Please. I was so lonely sitting here all by myself."

"We can't have that, now can we?" the man says as he sits on one side of me, the blonde on the other. The pixie-like brunette looks sheepish as she sits on the far side of the man.

"Black," the blonde says as she lifts my arm. "That's brave."

"Seems to be the color of the night," I say as I shoot one more glance over the couple I was originally watching.

"I guess they didn't have any plans to play tonight," the man whispers in my ear, both of us noticing their white bands.

"Lucky for us," the blonde says as her fingers release my wrist only to tease the neckline of my thin, satin top.

"Agreed," the man says as his fingers go in the opposite direction toward my bare thigh. "Are you interested in playing with us?"

That's the permission the guy in the front room was talking about, and I appreciate being asked. What makes cold chills rush over my skin is the fact that although I've dabbled in same-sex interaction in the past, they usually had more to do with turning a man on and thinking about his needs rather than what I actually wanted, and right now I just need to come. Call it selfish, but unless the pleasure is reciprocal, I don't have any interest.

"What did you have in mind?" I ask, my breaths rushing out when blondie pulls the front of my top forward and blows cool air over my heated skin.

"Amber here has been practicing her oral skills." He angles his head to indicate the brunette beside him. She gives me a sheepish smile. "Sydney can come if you just look at her right."

The blonde, Sydney, laughs on my other side.

"Lakin is right," Sydney confirms.

"So, she's not a very good barometer to use to evaluate Amber's skills," he continues, as do his wandering fingers on my skin. "So, we're looking for someone willing to test her tonight."

My eyes immediately find Amber's, and the lust is clear in her deep brown gaze. "Is that what you want?"

She nods, but I won't take the non-verbal consent as law.

"You want to make me come with your mouth?"

"Yes," she pants, and the immediate answer makes me wonder if it's just the idea of getting her tongue on me or if she's been played with some tonight to get her revved up.

"I'd love to help you guys out."

Hell, my thighs are already slick with anticipation. When she gets on her knees, Lakin grabs one of my legs while Sydney grabs the other. They spread me wide as each of them get the first look at my bare pussy.

I'm moaning just from her breath on me, and when her tongue strikes out at my clit the first time, I'm giving her an A+. I don't know if it's her skill level or the horny state I've been in for the last few weeks while trying to resist Kingston, but I'm coming after only a couple of short minutes.

As I come down, my hazy eyes look around the room. It's filled in some since the trio joined me, but it doesn't take long for me to find Kingston. As if he's forgotten why we're here, he's standing across the room, legs planted wide, cock in his hand.

I give him a weak smile before turning my attention back to my companions. Amber has already moved on from between my legs to Sydney's shaved snatch. The blonde squeals in delight before leaning across my body to take Lakin's cock in her mouth. Forced to change positions, Amber climbs off the floor before positioning Sydney over her mouth. Cool air from the room hits my over-heated pussy as they go to town on each other.

"Finger my girl," Lakin whispers in my ear before tugging down my satin top. Next, his mouth circles my nipple.

Sydney moans low in her throat when I reach over her ass and tease her opening with two fingers. Occasionally, Amber's lips wrap around them to suck them clean before she starts licking and nipping at Sydney's pussy.

Once again, my eyes find Kingston across the room. Only now, there's a woman on her knees in front of him. She's not close enough to suck on him, but there to catch his cum when he blows. I know he's close when his lips part, and even though he's at least fifteen feet away, I'm certain I can hear his grunt when the first spirt of semen hits her face. He never takes his eyes off me as rope after rope of cum jets from his cock.

My need for him, the same burning desire that has been eating me alive since I found out exactly who he is burns deep in my gut. I'm seconds away from pushing my play partners away so I can join him when my Latin stalker fills my vision.

Chapter 14

Max

I don't join the foursome immediately when I locate Jasmine on the sofa. Instead, I patiently sip my drink and watch from the settee across from them. Her pussy is proudly on display as the other three people get each other off. When the man comes, and the blonde also shakes in climax, they quickly excuse themselves.

"I feel bad for the brunette," I tell Jasmine as I approach her. "She seems to be the only one that didn't get to come."

"Lakin told me that the rest of the night is about her, so I imagine she'll have more fun than she can handle," she says as she closes her thighs, crossing her legs for good measure.

"Friends of yours?" I ask as I motion a request to join her.

She pats the sofa, so I sit.

"I just met them tonight."

Her voice is a little strained, but I choose to ignore it, hating that I got here after she'd already made her selection for the night. It doesn't help my plan if she's already finished.

"Are you done playing for the night?"

"Two weeks ago, you said you'd be right back. You disappeared," she says instead of answering my question, but now the reason for her irritation is clear.

"I got an urgent call and had to leave." The lie slips easily from my lips. "My apologies."

I lift her hand to my mouth and kiss the back of it.

"Forgive me?" I deepen my accent, knowing that she loves it to try to win her over.

"Depends on how you play your cards tonight."

Before I can assure her I'm an expert card player, the volume of the music grows louder. We turn our attention to the cage in the middle of the room, watching as a man and woman step inside. Next, they seduce each other in a dance clearly choreographed but sensual. Clothes begin disappearing as mouths and hands explore each other. The room is enthralled with the sight of them, but Jasmine seems distracted.

Then, she yawns wide, her hand barely making it to her mouth to cover it.

"You're tired," I say. "You should go home and get some rest."

"And leave your company?" She runs her hand down my chest, resting it lightly on my thigh. "Wouldn't dream of it. Besides, I live too far away."

"I have a hotel room nearby if you want to get a couple of hours of sleep," I offer, watching her face to see if she's going to think I'm moving too far, too fast. "The night is still young. We can always come back and play later."

"Or," her fingers on my thigh move over my crotch, brushing my semi, "we could just play at your place."

"Really?" I don't keep the shock out of my voice.

Her grip tightens on my dick as she licks her lips.

"I think it's a fabulous idea," she says. "Should we wait to see if King shows up? The three of us could have a lot of fun together."

"If he was coming, he'd be here by now." Honestly, I need to get her out of here before he does show up. "Come on."

I stand, offering her my hand, which she takes. There's a slight tremble in it, but it's to be expected. I'd be suspicious if she was gung ho about leaving a sex club with a man she hardly knows.

"Wait," the guy behind the counter says before we can leave the building. "I need a waiver signed."

"Waivers?" Jasmine asks as she turns back in his direction.

"Yep. Club rules. If you leave with someone you didn't arrive with, we have to get waivers saying that you're leaving of your own free will. It protects the club. I'm sure you understand."

Her eyes dart from mine to the clipboard in the guy's hand several times before she tucks her small clutch under her arm and reaches for it.

"You too," he tells me as he takes her sheet from the top and shoves the clipboard in my direction.

Jasmine huffs, and it makes me smile as I check the right boxes and sign my name.

"Sure takes the excitement out of the air, doesn't it?" she mumbles as the guy looks over our paperwork before going back behind his counter.

"Have a good night," he says. "Be safe."

Holding open the door for her, I feel the air change around us immediately when I step outside behind her. Not only is there someone in the parking lot, but they have plans for me. Needing to keep her close and safe, I press the palm of my hand to the small of her back. It will allow me to either pull her close or push her away if any real danger arrives.

My eyes dart to Jasmine, who walks close beside me with a tired look on her face. She doesn't notice the shadow creeping along the row of vehicles we're heading toward, but my body is coiled for war before the fist swings out to hit me.

With a quick shove against her back, I push her away a second before the fist hits my face. It doesn't stop the impact, but it keeps her from being in the middle.

When my head snaps back from the blow, I lock eyes with Kingston.

"You motherfucker," I growl before landing my fist against his face. With my head down and shoulders hard, I ram him in the gut before he can recover from my hit. We don't land on the ground as I'd planned, rather a car takes the brunt of our weight. My ground game has always been better than when I'm standing, and the vehicle being in the way keeps me from my objective.

With all of my power, I grab him and try to roll us free, but the sound of Jasmine's screams distracts me just long enough for Kingston to bring us back to standing. The one downfall with fighting this man is the fact that he knows most of my tricks from when we wrestled around as kids. I no longer have the element of surprise, but he also doesn't know how much fight training I've had. When I pull from a complicated hold, his eyes widen in shock. Jasmine screeches again when I pull my fist back and plow it into Kingston's face.

He grunts in pain, but like the man he has always been, he doesn't bother to reach up to his bleeding nose to assess the damage. He charges again, hitting me in the shoulder with the top of his head, and the forty or so pounds he has on me is enough to take us both to the ground.

Instead of pounding his fists into my face as I expect, he gains control of my arms, pinning them to the ground. Even in the heat of my anger, my cock jerks in my pants with him being on top of me like this. With his chest against mine and his legs straddling my hips, it's just like the many times I allowed myself the fantasy of him riding my cock, and fantasy is all it has ever been because there's no way Kingston fucking Jacks would allow me into him like that.

"Now," he seethes, but before I can open my mouth to ask him what he's talking about, I feel a sharp pinch in my arm.

Wondering if he's managed to pull a muscle in my shoulder, I look over seeing Jasmine with tears in her eyes as she pulls an empty syringe away.

"What the fuck?" I ask, but my words are already slowing, my brain going fuzzy.

My muscles loosen even when I urge them to fight against the man on top of me.

They don't listen, and soon after I can no longer hear.

It's seconds later when my eyes close and my world fades to black.

**

"What did you use?" I ask when I'm able to use my mouth again.

I haven't even opened my eyes yet, but I know my captors are close. I've done this myself more times than I can count, so I'm familiar with the drill.

"Etorphine," comes Kingston's husky answer.

"You could've fucking killed me," I hiss.

"That's still an option."

My eyes blink rapidly, but they remain hazy. When I lift my head, the first thing I see is Jasmine to the side. Her eyes are puffy from crying, but it's the bruise blooming on her cheek that makes me swivel my head looking for the asshole who ordered her to drug me.

"What the fuck?" I ask when he stalks toward me.

He's wearing a leather cut, the three-headed dog on the right side familiar. This has to be a joke.

"Why are you wear—"

"This?" he interrupts, using his thumb to lift the leather away from his neck. "It's simple, Carlos. If you have a beef with Cerberus, that means you have a beef with me."

My eyes widen. Not because he's implying that he's a member of the MC, but because I'd know it if he was.

"Did you miss that during your investigation of the club?" he taunts.

"The only info I could find was club names. There wasn't a King listed."

"My club name is Tug." He points to the other side of his cut.

I snort in derision, having no doubt why he was given that name.

"You need to start talking," he commands as he inches closer.

Lifting my hands to lunge for him, I discover I'm tied to a metal rack that's incomplete at the top. We're in some type of old hangar, and I'd bet my life that we're secluded and any hope of being overheard by someone willing to help me drains out of me.

"I won't say a word." It's only stubborn pride at this point keeping my lips closed.

Kingston being a member of Cerberus is an even better way to gain access than the woman is.

"Max," he warns. "Unless you want the beating of your life, I suggest you spill."

Chapter 15

Jasmine

Max?

Who the hell is Max?

I must gasp because both men snap their heads in my direction.

"She doesn't know about us?" the bound man says.

"Shut your fucking mouth," Kingston snarls. "Tell me what you want with Cerberus. Who are you helping to try and take down the club?"

"Max?" I mouth when the man keeps his eyes on me.

"Did he not tell you about our history?"

I shake my head, desperate for a clue about what is actually going on.

A loud crash jolts me, and I look over to find all the debris that was littering a table rolling across the floor. Kingston is pulling at his hair with his back to both of us, a string of expletives echoing around the room.

"He hasn't told you that we know each other? That we have a history?"

I shake my head.

"And he didn't tell you that he's known who I was for the last two weeks?"

"Max," Kingston warns again.

"Tell me what's going on," I insist, not caring who the information comes from. I just need the damn truth.

"It's a long story." He tries to lift his hands again but seems resigned to being tied up. "But it looks like we have nothing but time."

There's a taunting tone to his voice, and I have no doubt he's acting this way because it's the opposite of what Kingston wants.

"Kingston and I grew up in the same neighborhood," Max begins. "We were best friends until the summer before our senior year."

"And now you hate each other?" I ask.

"We didn't hate each other then," Max says. "We became even closer."

I look over at Kingston. He's leaning against the table with his thick arms crossed over his chest. His head is hung, eyes focused on the floor, and it pisses me off that he could've told me all of this shit at any point during the last two weeks he's spent in my apartment.

"The night before our first day of senior year, we kissed for the first time."

I keep my eyes on Kingston as Max tells of their history. His jaws ticks, but he refuses to look up. He seems resigned that Max is going to tell this story before he's willing to explain why he targeted the club.

"Mutual hand jobs happened in the second week of school. By Halloween our mouths had become very familiar with every inch of each other's body."

Kingston shifts his legs, uncrossing them at the feet to cross them the other direction, but he does nothing to hide the bulge forming at his groin.

"It wasn't until Christmas break that he had enough courage to ask if he could fuck me." Max chuckles as if he's still in that very memory. "I'd been waiting for him to ask, too scared to proposition him myself."

Kingston remains silent.

"We spent every possible moment together. We were best friends at school and lovers nearly every night. I didn't think life could get any better, but then he just up and left me."

My head swivels, expecting to find festering heartbreak on Max's face. Only he isn't looking at me, and he doesn't have sadness in his eyes. He's firing hatred toward Kingston's direction.

"I didn't just up and leave you," Kingston says, speaking for the first time since Max began his trip down memory lane. "You knew for months that I had to go."

"It was so easy for you to walk away," Max spits.

"You knew I couldn't stay!" Kingston roars as he pushes away from the table and rushes toward Max. His fist raises, and even though my hands fly to my mouth, preparing to watch another episode of violence, Max doesn't even blink.

"Because of your old man?" he asks. Max's eyes dart toward the hovering fist and then toward me. "Did you end up like him? Is that why she's going to have a black eye in the morning?"

"What?" Kingston asks, confused.

"Do you hit her like your dad hit your mom?"

My head is shaking, answering the questions even though it wasn't asked to me.

Kingston looks over his shoulder at me, but he doesn't lower his fist. He frowns, the lines between his eyes drawing in as if he's just now noticing the injury to the side of my face.

"You did that you piece of shit," he says when he snaps his face toward Max once again. "You clocked her when we were outside of *Hale-ish*."

Max's eyes dart to me again. Uncaring of the fist inches from his face, he looks at me with apology.

"It's okay," I tell him.

"It isn't," Kingston corrects.

"It wasn't purposeful. I would never hurt a woman."

"And you should know I wouldn't either." Kingston lowers his hand and shoves Max in the chest. With his tied position, Max doesn't move, but Kingston stalks away again, retaking his position against the table.

"Why did you fake your own death? Who are you working for? Why are you going after my club?" Kingston fires off a list of questions.

I want to know the answer to each of them, but I'm still reeling from the revelation that not only do these men know each other, but Kingston had every opportunity to tell me these things himself.

"Why didn't you tell me any of this?" Kingston looks up at me, but his lips stay sealed. "You've been in my apartment every single day for the last two weeks."

"Interesting," Max says with a playfulness to his tone that doesn't even begin to match the situation.

"Don't open your mouth again unless you plan to tell me what I want to know," Kingston tells him.

"I didn't know what he wanted. I still don't. There was no sense in me complicating things by telling you stuff that has no bearing."

"No bearing?" I snap, my fists opening and closing with the need to hit something, preferably Kingston's already bruised face.

"He was targeting me!" I point at my chest. "You knew who he was and didn't think I deserved that information?"

"I don't know what he wants!" he roars, pushing off the table to storm in my direction. "I was trying to keep you safe."

His voice softens as he draws closer.

"No." I hold my hands up before he can clasp them. "Don't use that placating voice thinking I'm just going to look into your eyes and forget that you've been lying to me for weeks."

"I didn't lie."

"Omission is still a lie," Max adds.

Kingston's jaw flexes so hard, I bet he's seconds away from splitting one of his back molars.

"Look at me," he says when I try to look over his shoulder.

Begrudgingly, my eyes find his. Even with all of my bluffing about not giving in to him, I do with record speed when he asks again.

"Telling you I knew who he is wouldn't have made any difference."

"You don't know that."

"I'm certain of it, because when I told you that the man who was going by Carlos at the club—" his voice lowers, "—the man who has been inside of you when I still haven't, was actually my best friend from childhood, Maximiliano Vazquez, you'd find the same thing I did."

I ignore the jab about us not having slept together. He seems a little bitter about the fact, bringing it up as often as he possibly can. You'd be surprised where he's able to insert that fact. He's become a master at inserting it into everyday conversation the last two weeks.

"And what is that?" I ask, my voice is just as low as his.

"That he died in a car accident ten years ago."

"What?" With hands on both of his shoulders, I try to shove him to the side to glare at Max, but I'm not strong enough.

On his own, Kingston steps aside, arms crossing over his chest as he turns to face his old friend with a smirk on his lips. I can't help but wonder if he's just told me this as a way to counterbalance what Max told me about Kingston breaking his heart.

"You let your best friend think you were dead for the last decade?" Max frowns, looking at Kingston, not me. "Who the hell does that?"

Unable to be still any longer, I jump off the table I've been sitting on and brush past Kingston.

"Is that what this is?" I ask Max when he doesn't offer anything up. "Are you going after Cerberus because you're bitter about Kingston breaking your heart when you were kids?"

Max keeps his eyes on Kingston, refusing to look in my direction.

"I'm talking to you, Maximiliano Vazquez," I spit, stepping right in front of his face so he's forced to look at me.

"Maximiliano Vazquez is dead. You can call me Special Agent Rodrigo Flores."

Chapter 16

Tug

"FBI? No fucking way."

I'm talking more to myself than challenging what Max just said.

"Do you think some kid from small-town USA would be able to fake his own death and make it believable?" Max challenges.

I wouldn't even let myself consider the possibility weeks ago when I discovered Carlos was, in fact, Max. My friend was always in too much trouble as a kid, and extensive background checks for any government agency would produce his juvenile history, no matter that he was told they'd be sealed if he stayed out of trouble.

"So that means the FBI is interested in Cerberus?"

Jasmine immediately shakes her head as she glares at Max. "Impossible."

He doesn't speak to her or answer my question, rather he looks at me and asks, "How long have you been with them?"

"Long enough to fucking know they work *with* the FBI not against them."

He turns his eyes back to Jasmine, and I'm seconds away from hitting him in the mouth again. I hate his eyes on her, especially when I still don't know what his end goal is.

"I'm not here to hurt you, and it was never my intention to scare you." He swallows, his eyes shifting to mine before going back to her. "I need your help."

"You're trying to tell me that you targeted her in a sex club to ask her for help?" I shake my head vigorously. If he's just going to keep lying, I might as well beat his ass. I have another syringe waiting for the ride back to the clubhouse. We can take him there and let Kincaid figure out what to do with his ass.

"I couldn't just go to the club directly, again."

"Again?" Jasmine asks before I can open my mouth to do so.

"I emailed them more than once. They told me to go to my superiors, that I didn't have the clearance to request things of them."

"What exactly were you asking for?"

Max's eyes find mine, and tears I never expect pool on his lashes. This isn't going to be good at all. He was never an emotional man, and even with training, there's no way he's faking the emotion that's crushing him right now.

"Mia. I need help finding Mia."

"Mia?" My knees weaken, and I stumble back a foot before I catch myself from collapsing to the ground.

"Who is Mia?" Jasmine asks. "Was she your third in high school? The girl you guys shared like you did with me?"

Both Max and I cringe at the implication.

"She's my sister," Max says just as I say, "She's like a sister to me."

Some form of relief washes over her, and I plan on revisiting that little emotion of hers at some point, but now is not the time.

"Who has her?"

"I don't know."

"Why did they take her?"

"I don't know that either."

"What the fuck do you know, Max!"

"Don't yell at him," Jasmine yells as she tries to shove me out of the way to get to him. She tries to pull the zip ties from his wrists, but they're the thick industrial ones, and without a knife she'll never be able to get him loose. "Untie him."

I ignore her demand. "Not yet."

"Not yet? Look at him." She jabs her finger in his direction. "He doesn't want to hurt us; he needs our help."

"I heard what he said. Forgive me if I don't trust you just yet."

Max nods, his government training allowing him to understand my position.

"Explain," I urge.

Max clears his throat before he begins, "I was warned a million times, instructed to stay away from everyone I knew in my past life when the FBI recruited me — joining as Max wasn't a possibility. My criminal record kept that from happening. When I was approached, it wasn't because they saw me as having potential as an agent but because I had been busted for cybercrimes. Someone, somewhere, saw potential in me. They offered me a job, gave me the terms of how they would make that happen, and it only took me about ten minutes to decide."

"So, they would give you a new identity and all you had to do was die and destroy your family?" I ask, not hiding the venom in my voice. "Destroy me?"

"You weren't even part of my consideration," he says emotionless. "I knew going to prison would cause just as much pain, bring just as much shame to my family. So, I made the decision to die. Working for the FBI sounded like an amazing plan to twenty-one-year-old me."

"And how has that worked out for you?" I spit. He sure as fuck doesn't seem happy, especially with the knowledge that his twin sister has been abducted.

"Walking away was harder than I expected. It was impossible for me not to see my family —" His eyes lower to his lap. "To see all the people, I cared for. When surveillance through FBI channels wasn't enough, I made trips, always staying on the periphery, keeping to the shadows."

My skin crawls with memories, or what I thought at the time were figments of my imagination after training too long and not getting enough sleep.

"Did you come to California?"

Max gives me a weak smile. "As I said, I had a hard time staying away from the people I care for."

Care, present tense, not past. My heart kicks in my chest.

"You went to see him?" Jasmine asks for clarification.

"Several times," Max confesses.

We'll have time to talk about his need to be a complete asshole later. Right now, we need to focus on Mia.

"You don't know who took Mia?" I ask again to get us back on track. "Or know why she was taken?"

That information could lead us to her abductors.

"I think I was made during one of my trips back home," he says. "I don't think they knew who she was to me, but just that she was someone important."

"She'll know by now. If they have half a brain, they will show her a picture and demand information after she had no knowledge of SA Rodrigo Flores."

"Which puts her in even more danger," Max adds.

"Can you cut him loose now, please?" Jasmine asks again.

"Why does the FBI need Cerberus's help?"

"They don't. I do. My superiors refused to look into it, and when I didn't stop digging, they fired me."

"Fired you?" I snap. "That doesn't make any sense. Ten years of resources and training an agent just doesn't get tossed away that easily."

"Exactly," Max mutters. "I was told they'd resurrect me and lock me up for the cybercrimes they originally busted me for if I didn't just drop it. I can't do shit for Mia in prison, but I also can't just walk away when my sister could be anywhere suffering from God knows what."

"Completely understandable," Jasmine agrees before turning her burning eyes back in my direction. "Untie him."

Sure that he's telling the truth, I pull my knife from my pocket and make easy work of the zip ties holding Max in place. His fingers automatically go to his wrists, rubbing them back and forth.

"I don't understand my dad or Uncle Diego turning you down," Jasmine says as she puts some distance between herself and Max.

I'm sure he won't hurt her, but she's smart to remain cautious.

"I wasn't able to give them all the information. I actually lied to them when I told them I was still with the Bureau. I already risked going to prison, knowing if they reached out to my superiors they would come looking for me," Max says with a sigh as he stands from the chair and stretches. "Hell, I've been keeping a low profile for the last month in fear that they were already looking for me."

"A month?" I hiss. "How long has she been gone?"

"Six weeks," he answers.

"You have to consider the fact that she's alr—"

"Don't," Max warns. "I won't even let myself think that way, and you better not fucking speak of it. Mia is alive, and I need help getting her back."

"We can speak to Kincaid about it. Blade should be able to narrow down the search."

"Blade is who I went to in the first place," Max says. "All I really need is a secure network. I'm certain Cerberus has all the same facial recognition software that the FBI has."

I don't confirm his suspicions, but Jasmine looks back at me with a hopeful look in her eyes.

"We have to help him."

"We can ask," I repeat. "Let's go."

"Delilah and Lawson are getting married tomorrow," Jasmine reminds me.

"That just means everyone will be at the clubhouse. It's easier to approach the entire team. It's harder for them to turn us down," I say as I walk toward the door to leave the building.

"Us?" Jasmine squeaks.

Max chuckles at her reaction, and a frown forms on my lips. I don't look forward to the next twenty-four hours, but finding Mia is my only priority. If facing Dominic over what's been going on with his daughter is something I have to deal with to get there, I'll do it with a smile on my face.

Chapter 17

Jasmine

The whole ride back, Max and Kingston argued over where he was going to stay when we got back to Farmington. My live-in bodyguard wasn't happy when I offered my apartment.

"This is a terrible idea," Kingston huffs as he unlocks the door to my apartment.

Shortly after arriving two weeks ago, he made himself a key and came and went like he owned the place.

"Cozy," Max says as he steps inside.

"I'm beat," I tell them, heading down the hall toward my room.

Let them figure out where they're sleeping tonight. All I want is to wash my face and climb under my soft sheets. I'm not built for this kind of action.

After brushing my teeth and getting my makeup off, I leave the bathroom only to hear the guys arguing in the living room. I listen without shame while I take off my clothes and replace them with a thin, thigh-length camisole.

"If anyone is sleeping in her bed it'll be me," Kingston says.

"Looks like you haven't spent any time in there so far," Max counters.

"How the fuck would you know? I've been here for two weeks."

"And sleeping on the couch from the looks of the folded sheets over there."

I smile, loving how much both of them pay attention to detail. I also know Kingston has been standing outside of my bedroom door waiting to hear the click of my vibrator every damn night since the first time he stayed here. What he doesn't know is that I've been carrying it in my purse and taking a few moments to myself in my car after work. I don't do it in the college parking lot, of course. I have no desire to end up in jail, but there's a gravel road between school and the clubhouse, and I make that turnoff every day before heading over for my swim.

"There's no way you're going to just show up and invite yourself to sleep in her bed."

"Where do you think we were heading before you jumped me, asshole?"

"You must not be a very good agent if you haven't figured out that she was in on the plan."

Silence fills the room, and I angle my head further to try to hear better.

"You're an asshole for that, Kingston. My head still fucking hurts from that fucking injection."

Grinning, I walk down the hallway to find them chest to chest just glaring at each other. I wonder if suggesting they fuck the anger out of each other would go over well.

"Max?" He turns his head to look at me as I hold out my hand. His eyes skate up and down my body, settling on my tits. "I have some painkillers in my room."

With a smirk, as if he's won the competition, Max clasps my hand and follows me back to my room. Just before I leave the living room, I turn back and toss Kingston a quick wink.

"Motherfucker," he spits.

"You're going to make him crazy," Max says as I pop the top of the maximum-strength headache medicine.

"I know."

He smiles wide before popping the pills in his mouth and taking the bottle of water I lift from my bedside table.

"Is it hard seeing him again after so long?"

"Probably not as hard as it is for him to see me," he confesses. "I lived on pins and needles each time he shipped out for duty. I can't imagine what it would be like to hear about his death. I don't think I'd be able to live if that ever happened."

"You still love him."

"Not by choice," he grumbles with a quick kiss to my temple before turning toward the door.

"Where are you going?"

"Back out there." He hitches his thumb over his shoulder.

"I was hoping you'd stay here with me."

He cocks an eyebrow at me. "Are you trying to get in between us?"

There's a hint of warning in his tone, one that tells me he'd never allow it, but at the same time, a little smile is tugging at the corner of his mouth, like he's willing to play along for a little while.

"I've been trying to get between you guys for weeks," I tell him saucily, "but that isn't going to happen tonight. I'm beyond exhausted, but that far side of the bed is yours if you want it."

I fall on to my regular side of the bed as Max turns out the light and crawls in beside me. Like a gentleman, he doesn't touch me, and it doesn't take long before my eyes flutter closed, and sleep overtakes me.

"Scoot."

I feel a nudge on my side.

"Jasmine, scoot over."

Kingston's husky voice rouses me from sleep enough that I obey. The warmth of his body is too damn enticing to resist, so I snuggle against his chest and fall back asleep.

***

"You didn't waste any time," Max says with a whisper.

I have to be laying on Kingston because the chest under me doesn't rumble when Max speaks.

"Mind your own fucking business," Kingston returns as his arm tightens around my back.

"You have feelings for her." There's pain in Max's voice, and it makes me feel like an asshole.

These men belong together. They wear their love for each other on their damn sleeves. No matter how much they want people on the outside to think differently, I watched how they would look back and forth at each other on the drive back last night. The longing and need in their eyes made me wish someone would look at me that way. It made me realize what I have been missing.

I never wanted a relationship, knowing one single man would never be able to give me what I wanted. Plus, commitment to someone meant that playing with others would eventually become a thing of the past, even if things started differently. I wasn't in a place to give that up, but with the heat of Kingston's chest under me and the warmth of Max's body behind me, maybe this was enough.

"She gets my dick hard," Kingston grunts in response to Max's accusation.

Not the declaration I was hoping for.

"I get your dick hard," Max counters, "and you have feelings for me."

"Do not," Kingston argues.

"I don't get your dick hard, or you don't have feelings for me?"

"Neither."

Kingston Jacks is a liar. His cock is hard against my leg right now.

"Why don't you just pull your cocks out, so we can measure and see whose is bigger," I grumble against Kingston's chest. "That way, you two can stop arguing like little boys fighting over a toy."

"That's a great plan," Max says as he grips my shoulder to tug me back a few inches.

Kingston's arm doesn't release me, and Max, not one to give up so easily just scoots closer, his own erection digging into my back.

"Mine's bigger," Kingston says. "We've measured them before."

"Of course, you have." I chuckle.

Max's hand creeps under Kingston's arm to get to my breast.

"This okay?" he asks, pinching my nipple between his fingers.

"Mmm," I respond.

"This is so fucked up, Jasmine."

My cheeks heat when Kingston speaks. Maybe debauchery is okay in the club, but in my room in the light of the morning sun coming through the blinds, what I crave isn't allowed.

Before I can get lost in my own head, Max pulls me back as Kingston rolls out from under me. Instead of climbing off the bed, he climbs over me, Max's hand sweeping my camisole up just in time for the heat of Kingston's boxer covered cock to settle against my clit.

"I've spent two weeks in this apartment needing to fuck you, and you turned me down every damn time. One night just sleeping in this bed with Max and you get all hot and bothered, letting him touch your perfect fucking tits like they belong to him."

"She likes me more," Max teases, his mouth working magic on my neck.

"He takes what he wants," I pant when the man on top of me flexes his hips, digging his cock harder against me. "He doesn't beg like a little boy. He doesn't ask permission. He just expects me to want exactly what he has to give."

"Is that right?" Kingston asks, his eyes growing darker.

"Mm-hmm," I answer, unable to form actual words.

"And if I do the same?"

I swallow thickly. "Then I'll probably come from three thrusts of your cock inside of me."

"Jesus," he moans as he reaches to his waist to push his boxers down as Max pulls my panties to the side. "Is that right?"

The heat of his skin on mine is better than anything I've ever felt before in my life.

"So if I just—" He swirls the head of his dick in my arousal before pressing the first bare inch inside of me.

"Goddamn, that's hot," Max mutters, lifting my leg closest to him further out so he can get a better look.

Kingston's eyes burn me as he pushes his hips forward, sinking slowly all the way inside of me. Surprisingly, he isn't watching our connection like Max is. His eyes are on mine. I nod my head, no clue what I'm giving him permission for, but he seems to understand something even if I don't.

"Jasmine." My name is an invocation on his lips, but before I can close my eyes and just let the sensations take over my body, banging comes from my front door.

"The fuck?" Kingston hisses as he pulls out of me.

Max bites his lip as I whimper from Kingston's loss. "Don't stop. Just keep going."

When I look over, I notice Max has taken the opportunity to pull his own cock out of his boxers, and even as the knocking continues, so does his hand as he strokes his dick.

"She doesn't get visitors," Kingston says as he climbs off the bed and pulls up his jeans sans boxers. I almost cry as his cock disappears behind the denim.

"It's probably the mailman with a delivery." Max nods enthusiastically as if he'll convince Kingston to get right back in bed. "He'll leave it in the hall if you don't answer."

"It's Sunday," Kingston and I mutter at the same time.

I jump off the bed, pulling my robe on and tying it tight around my waist.

"Jasmine!"

"Fuck," I hiss as I walk into the hallway. "It's my sister. Grab those sheets off the couch and get your stuff out of here. Don't come out of my room."

Kingston moves into action, taking less than thirty seconds to do as I asked before he disappears into my room.

"What took so damn long?" Sophia asks in lieu of hello when I open the door.

"I was asleep," I lie.

She steps inside, but before I can close the door, Camryn pops her head in the doorway, followed by Gigi and Ivy.

"I'm pretty sure you have more important things to do on your wedding day than come to my apartment," I tell Delilah just as I'm wrapping my arms around her for a long hug.

"Hey," my sister whines. "You saw her this summer. I haven't seen you since Christmas last year."

My sister tugs Delilah away from me for a hug.

"Not my fault you didn't come home this summer."

"If you met Callum, you'd understand why I spent the summer backpacking around Europe with him rather than hanging out in New Mexico," my sister informs me before taking a deep breath and scrunching her nose. "I thought you said you were sleeping."

"I was." I pull my hair over my shoulder and sniff it.

"You smell like sex."

The other girls chuckle.

"I wish," I tell my sister, hoping she'll fall for the tone of my voice.

"Who is here with you?"

"No one," I answer a little too fast.

"Nope," Camryn says, grabbing Sophia by the shoulders just before she can get my bedroom door open. "Not your business."

"I'm her sister. Of course, it's my business."

"There's no one in there."

"Then why is the door closed?" Her eyes narrow on me, but Camryn still has a grip on her shoulders. Thankfully, Gigi and Ivy have taken a position between the door and her.

"I didn't know who was at the door. My room's a mess. I don't want visitors to see it like that."

"You were supposed to be at the clubhouse last night when I got home," Sophia complains. She's always been good about making me feel bad.

It won't work this time. Max and helping find his sister Mia are worth a little lost time with my own sister.

"Why are you girls here so early?" I ask, ignoring my sister.

She huffs, but I can tell there isn't any real ire in her actions because she's still trying to work out what I'm hiding from her.

"We're on our way to the spa," Delilah says.

Just the mention of the spa makes me miss what started in my room fifteen minutes ago. Camryn narrows her eyes on mine before they pop open and sparkle with humor. She's got a clue. We've had more than one conversation about *Hale-ish* and the other clubs I've gone to. She hasn't been brave enough to ask Samson to take her yet, but I imagine she'll build up the courage soon.

"Why don't you ladies wait in the limo downstairs," Camryn suggests.

Gigi, Ivy, and Delilah inch toward the front door, but Sophia's legs are planted.

"Whatever you have to say can be said in front of all of us," my sister hisses.

She and Camryn haven't spent any time with each other since Samson and she became a couple. All she knows of Camryn is being the strict babysitter from her childhood, and now as she tries to establish her independence in adulthood, she sees this as a fight she's going to win.

"We're going to talk about old lady stuff, like hiding lumps under spandex for the wedding," Camryn says with practiced ease.

"So stupid," Sophia huffs, but she lets Gigi guide her out the door.

"I don't need that back," Gig says just before she leaves.

I follow her finger to the monarch butterfly mask on the side table where I dropped it with my purse. She laughs as the door shuts because right beside my mask is Kingston's and Max's.

"Two!" Camryn hisses when the door clicks closed. "You little minx."

I press my fingers to her lips, but she shoves them away.

"I noticed the masks when we first walked in, but it wasn't until Sophia said you smelled like sex that I knew for sure."

"I need to ask you a favor."

She shakes her head no before I can even finish. "You can't skip out on Delilah just to have kinky sex with two men."

My thighs clench at the implication. "That's not what I was going to ask. I'm going to the spa with you, but I'm going to need some time after the ceremony."

"And why do you need my help?"

I smile. "Everyone will be there, and I just need a little warning in case I'm about to get caught."

"Tell me exactly what you need," she offers.

Two minutes later, Camryn is leaving with the assurance she'll have them hold the car for me, so I can get dressed.

When I open the door to my bedroom, I expect to find the guys hiding in my closet not to be discovered.

Instead, the sight of them in a sixty-nine position, sucking each other off is ten times better.

"Wanna join?" Max says as he pops his mouth off Kingston's cock.

He doesn't have time to say much more because the former Marine urges his mouth back over his length. My core quivers seconds later when King grunts his release. Max isn't long behind him as the bigger guy doubles his efforts.

"Holy shit," I mutter.

Both men look over at me, lips glistening with the other's release.

"Your turn," Max says as he climbs off the bed with a grin.

"Hold that thought." I hold up my hands to ward him off. "I have bridesmaids' duties today, but after the ceremony, and hopefully getting the news you need about getting help finding Mia, we can meet up later at the clubhouse."

Both men groan at my rejection, and I get dressed and out of there as fast as I can. Just the scent in the air surrounding them is enough to make me want to throw the deadbolt on the door and ignore the rest of the world.

Chapter 18

Tug

"I only did that because I didn't want to have achy balls all day," I tell Max as we climb in the SUV, ready to head to Cerberus.

"Liar. You did it because you wanted to. You could've jacked off in the shower if you didn't want blue balls," he snaps as I put the vehicle in drive.

He has always called me on my shit, and it seems even thirteen years later he's fallen right back into the task. I keep my focus off the man beside me and on the road, refusing to confirm what we both know.

Silence fills the SUV as we make our way across town toward the Cerberus clubhouse. Everything that we need to say but are avoiding fills the distance between us until it's so big and heavy I fear it'll swallow us whole before we hit the property.

Small talk was never our style, so neither one of us travel down that path, but when I chance a look over at him, I find his eyes glued to my lips. Arousal renews in my gut. Years ago, we were insatiable with each other, taking risks on getting caught fooling around at school, the local diner, and any other place we could find a few moments together.

I wish I could chalk his obsession with my mouth up to his desire for my lips to be wrapped around his dick again, and that's definitely part of his focus, but I also know the connection we have, the one we've always had. It's like I never walked away. It's like he's longed for me every second, like I've longed for him. The only difference is while I was grieving the loss of him and beating myself up for all the things I did wrong and the things I never had the courage to say, he was keeping tabs on me. He had every chance to step out of the fucking shadows and tell me the truth. He didn't have to let his death linger in my blood like a disease, eating me from the inside out. Yet, he did.

His absence tortured me, his parents, and his twin sister. As happy as I am that he isn't gone, I don't know that I can ever forgive him for making that choice.

"How do you think this is going to go?" he asks with uncertainty as I park the SUV in the Cerberus parking lot.

He's stalling. I recognize the tactic.

"I'm not sure."

It's the most honest truth I can give him. I've worked with Cerberus for the last year, only having taken a few weeks to myself after discharging from the Corps, but I don't know how the structure works exactly. I know there's a guy named Blade in New England that routes the jobs and information to us, but I'm not privileged as to how he gets the missions set up. Honestly, I never even thought to ask. Just like in the Corps, I follow orders. We're part of a team, but it's not my responsibility to set things up. They'd probably tell me if I asked. It's not like we're on a need-to-know basis, but I trust them to make sure we're as prepared as we can possibly be before we leave town on a mission.

"I imagine they'll help."

At least, I hope they will.

"They turned me down once before."

"They told you to speak with your superiors," I clarify. "That's not the same thing."

"Let's go," I urge, opening the door to the vehicle.

A shiver runs down my spine from the cutting December wind, and I wrap my jacket tighter around me.

"How did you end up here?" Max asks as we make our way across the parking lot. "Do they have an online application process or something?"

I can't help the chuckle that slips out. "They recruited me. I didn't even know about Cerberus when I discharged. I just knew that making a career out of my enlistment wasn't what I wanted anymore. I loved the work, but there was something about walking away and having some level of freedom that pulled me more."

"So you—?"

I hold my hand up to silence him before I open the door. If he wanted to know all of these things about me, he could've come to me sooner. He doesn't get the right to fill in the last thirteen years at his whim.

"We can talk about it later. Right now, we need to focus on getting Mia home."

I won't tell him about the dream I had last night, and even if we find her alive, that she may still wish she was dead. Even after all the support and resources provided by Cerberus and many other outreach groups around the world, the women we bring home are never the same. I can't stop my mind from thinking of Colby Davis. She was the daughter of a Hollywood power couple. It only took a week after being rescued that she downed a bottle of pain pills because she couldn't take living in a world filled with such treachery. She was one of seven rescued by Cerberus that day. I didn't participate during that mission because I was still in the service, but it struck home when I heard about it on the news because of the crush I'd had on the young starlet.

Many more of our missions than should end that way. I'm not bitter. I've never sat and thought we were wasting our time and chancing our own lives to rescue women who come home and commit suicide; rather I keep my focus on the ones who come home and live as normal lives as they can. Their new normal.

"Kingston?"

I forgot that I'm standing on the front porch with my hand on the doorknob until Max places his hand on my shoulder. At this moment, I hate the cold air and the thickness of my leather jacket and the cut underneath because I can't feel the warmth of his hand. I hate that I'll never be able to prepare him for what we may find when we dig deeper into Mia's case. I can't open my mouth to form the words that even if we do get her home safely, that it's the torment in her mind and not those that hurt her that could be the final nail in her coffin. Survival is just that. Living with the terror afterward is what's difficult.

"Let's go," I grunt, pulling the door open and stepping across the threshold.

"Hey," Scooter says from a ladder on the other side of the room. He's helping a couple of the other guys hang garland along the rafters.

"It looks like a winter wonderland in here," Max says, and I can hear the awe in his voice.

"A Cerberus wedding is a big deal," Rocker says as he makes his way toward us with his hand out toward Max. "Rocker. Are you Tug's date for the wedding?"

Date?

My eyes widen, and it takes all the energy I have not to wipe at my mouth to check if I have cum on my lips from earlier.

"This is M—"

"Rodrigo Flores," Max interrupts, clasping Rocker's hand. "Old friend from back home. He's too ugly to date."

Rocker laughs, but the look in his eyes is telling. He's a smart fucker, and the simple explanation hasn't done anything to ease his suspicions.

"Welcome to the clubhouse." Rocker sweeps his arm toward the room. "The wedding has been a long time coming, and the after-party is going to be epic. Make sure you stick around."

We both watch Rocker walk toward a table filled with decorations. Even without the extra lighting plugged in that some of the guys are working on, the room sparkles in whites, silvers, and a frosty turquoise. Every inch of the room glows with happiness, both in the decorations as well as the people who are all making it come together. I don't know Delilah or Lawson very well at all, but I can feel the love in the room as people work diligently to make their fairytale wedding come true.

"That's Kincaid," I tell Max, pointing subtly across the room. "Let's go."

His arm clutches mine, and if I didn't feel the fear of rejection thrumming through his touch, I'd shrug him off. Too much is already being questioned with Rocker's words. The last thing I need is my crew wondering about my sexuality. I shake my head to ward off those thoughts. Snatch and Itchy have been together forever, and none of the guys have a problem with their relationship, but my initial instinct is to deny, deny, deny.

"It's fine," I assure Max, gently touching his hand before pulling my arm away.

His eyes burn with the rejection, but I walk forward to greet my boss with a handshake.

"So formal, Tug. Who's this?" His tone is calm and welcoming, but his eyes are assessing the situation before I can even get the words out. "Not exactly how we do things but let me get the guys together."

Max clears his throat as Kincaid taps out a text on his phone. Notification sounds echo around the room as the guys stop working to check their phones.

"This way," Kincaid says, walking toward the large meeting room in the center of the clubhouse. Cerberus members all around us stop what they're doing and make their way in behind us.

"Not intimidating at all," Max mutters as we stand to the side while all the others take their seats. Shadow was already in the room typing on his laptop, but we wait a few extra moments because a few of the guys are lagging.

"Sorry we're late," Snatch says as he tumbles into the room with Itchy right behind him.

Several of the guys chuckle when Itchy wipes his hand over his beard. "Wedding jitters."

"Lawson or Delilah?" Kid asks with a knowing smirk.

"Me," Snatch mumbles.

Another chuckle echoes around the room, but the second Kincaid clears his throat, everyone settles.

I ignore the questioning look Max gives me. I know he wants to ask me about the two men, and about why every single Marine in this room is okay with their relationship. My perspective from all those years ago was that being anything other than straight in the Marine Corps wasn't a possibility. I don't have the energy to explain that maybe I was wrong.

"You have the floor, Tug," Kincaid says as he takes a seat at the head of the table.

"My friend, M—"

"Rodrigo Flores," Max interrupts again.

I frown at him, giving my head a slight shake. His eyes fill with terror when he realizes that I won't lie to these guys. We're brothers, if not by blood then by the experiences we've all shared. I won't give them half-truths and tell them lies.

"This is Special Agent Rodrigo Flores," I explain, and relief washes over him.

No one moves. They aren't strangers to meeting men from different agencies. I was only shocked at the discovery because I couldn't reconcile my friend from school being an agent.

"He's also an old friend from school, Maximiliano Vazquez."

"You reached out to Blade a couple of weeks ago," Shadow says, his fingers flying over the keyboard on his laptop. He doesn't even look toward us as he speaks.

"Yes." Max swallows a lump in his throat before continuing, "I wasn't completely truthful with him."

"So, you didn't bother to tell him you were separated from the FBI?"

Kincaid's eyes narrow.

"No."

"His sister has been abducted," I say, once again jumping in to save his ass like I did a hundred times when we were kids.

Max glares at me, his pride not allowing him to be grateful. "The FBI wouldn't help."

"Because the men who took your sister are under investigation from four different agencies," Shadow says, his fingers still flying over the keys. I'm not at all surprised how fast he's pulling up this information. It's what he's always done. "They have eleven agents undercover in a three-year operation. Your sister isn't the only one in trouble."

The room grows silent.

"What?" Max asks. "Who is the focus of the investigation?"

Shadow's eyes find Max's, but rather than answering him, he looks at Kincaid.

These men have been a team for decades, and it's with that closeness that they have a conversation, tons of information are computed, all without a word being said.

"Luis—"

"Cortez?" Scooter snarls like he has a personal vendetta against the man they spent the last two weeks in South America tracking down.

"Jiménez," Kincaid corrects, his jaw working back and forth. It's the only outward sign that he's annoyed with Scooter's outburst.

"The Colombia drug lord?" Max asks.

Kincaid nods before angling his head back to Shadow, giving him the floor once again.

"He's not only into drugs and guns, but he's now into trafficking women."

Max's face drains of blood, and it's Rocker who guides him to a chair to sit down.

"The FBI isn't willing to blow a three-year sting operation for your sister."

Max's shoulders rack with sobs he doesn't bother to hide. Several of the men around the table grow restless in their chairs. They aren't liking the information we're being given any more than Max does.

"You were my last hope," Max says, emotion making his words come out in rough jabs.

"I said the FBI wasn't willing to help," Shadow says with a pointed look.

A couple of guys down at the end of the table let out a whoop, but Max just looks around confused. He doesn't understand that Shadow just confirmed that even though the other agencies are involved, we also have a job to do. It won't be the first time we had to step on a few toes to complete a mission.

Chapter 19

Jasmine

"You're not going to tell me who it is?" Camryn whispers as she straightens the strap of my gown.

I roll my lips between my teeth, not because I don't want to answer her, but my sister's ears perk up each time our heads get close to each other. We've been trying to talk all day, but there are so many people around we haven't been able to speak much.

"You really that interested in my sex life?"

"I'm more curious to know which Cerberus guy goes to that sex club," she says conspiratorially.

"Why?" I pull my head back, ready to jump her ass. "Is Samson not enough for you?"

Her brows pinch together. "That's a really narrow-minded thing to say considering you had two men in your apartment this morning, but I'm not looking for fun on the side. Samson is everything to me. He's all I'll ever need."

"Sorry," I mumble. "I didn't mean to judge even if that's what you guys were into."

"Apologize by telling me who it is," she bargains with an eyebrow raised.

"Who do you think it is?" I ask.

"I imagine Scooter." She looks around the room to make sure no one is listening in before turning back in my direction. "I heard he's into anal."

"Who isn't?" I ask with a wink.

We both giggle like preteens.

"So, it's Scooter?"

I shake my head.

"Please tell me it isn't Jameson. I know Gigi is wild, but I can't see her letting him stay at your house. If he was the one in your room, I imagine she'd be right there with him."

"No!" I hiss, drawing the attention of several of the other girls.

"What are you two over here gossiping about?" Sophia says with her hands on her hips as she steps up beside Camryn.

"Nothing," we both say a little too quickly.

"Yeah, sure," my sister mutters before walking away.

I feel terrible for leaving her out of this, but adult or not, I'm uncomfortable discussing my sex life with her. It's just not going to happen.

"So, about that time I need later?" I remind Camryn.

"I'll make sure everyone stays away from the rooms," she assures me.

I know I'll have to tell her eventually, but now isn't the time.

"Everyone ready?" Emmalyn asks as she steps inside the meeting room.

It was the only place big enough for all of us to get ready.

We all nod our agreement, lining up in the order she put us in earlier during practice. Each one of the women lined up behind me is being paired off with their significant others. Ivy is Delilah's maid of honor, and she looks stunning in her silver dress. Mine, Gigi's, and Camryn's are an icy turquoise coordinating perfectly with the decorations all the Cerberus guys helped put up earlier.

"You ready?" Cannon asks as he steps up beside me with his arm curved.

"Such a gentleman," I whisper as we wait for the music to start.

He hums his agreement, but then his eyes skate down my neck to my chest. Shame swallows me halfway down the aisle when my nipples furl against the satin of my dress. In my hustle out of the apartment today, I managed to leave my strapless bra, so I knew just how easy it was for everyone to see the arousal I can't hide. I also left unsatisfied and needy, which explains how this smirking boy on my arm has the ability to arouse me.

Before walking away, Cannon presses a friendly kiss to my temple, and instead of watching the young man stand to the side, I turn my attention back to the aisle in time to watch Gigi and Jameson walking toward the front. I know it's only a matter of time before they're the one at the end of the procession, with her in a gorgeous white dress.

Camryn and Samson are next, followed by Ivy and Griffin. My lips turn up in a genuine smile seeing all these people I grew up with dressed in such elegant clothes.

Just as the music changes and Delilah begins to walk toward her soon-to-be groom, my eyes land on Kingston in the audience. If I thought the people I grew up with cleaned up nicely, none of them have a thing on this man. In dark slacks and a button-down shirt, he's so handsome. The way his shirt sleeves are rolled up, his forearms give a tiny hint to the sexual-being under the nice fabrics.

He winks at me, but before I can respond, Camryn is tugging my arm and urging me to turn around. I feel his gaze on my back during the entire ceremony.

Weddings have never been my thing, but there's something magical about the coming together of two people who love each other beyond the realm of explanation. Lawson and Delilah prepared their own vows, and although they were filled with inside stories and jokes I didn't understand, their love outshined any confusion I might have had from their words.

Pure joy and ecstatic energy swells in the room when they kiss for the first time as husband and wife. Delilah giggles as she pulls away as Lawson inches in closer for one more sip at her lips. Ruckus applause and cheers break out when they turn and face their guests with their hands clasped and wide smiles on each of their faces.

Jaxson and Rob held each other, both with tears running down their red faces when instead of walking directly back down the aisle, Lawson and Delilah stopped to hug each of them.

When they disappeared down the hallway, Emmalyn and Misty ushered everyone to the kitchen to eat. The overly large room fit all guests comfortably with room to spare since it was only close friends, family, and the Cerberus guys. I avoided looking in Kingston's direction, and he must've explained things to Max because even though the man winked at me once, he kept his distance.

"Beautiful ceremony," my dad says as he walks closer and places a buttered roll on top of my nearly empty plate.

"Yes," I agree. "Delilah made for a gorgeous bride."

"You'll be even prettier when I walk you down the aisle."

I roll my eyes at him. I know he's only half-serious, about me getting married not about being gorgeous. I don't have self-esteem issues that require frequent praise, but he's grown used to the idea that I may never get married. At twenty-five, I told him I had no interest in traditional ties to a man, but he just reminded me that he didn't find his true love until he was almost forty, so I still had time for my knight to show up.

"You want to sit with us?" Dad asks when I look over to see the table with the other bridesmaids full.

My eyes sweep over the room, and even though there's a spot at Kingston's table, I follow my dad to join my mother already sitting at the table.

"Weddings always make me sentimental," Khloe says as I sit beside her. "Don't they make you the same way?"

Dustin kisses the back of her hand, and when he gives her a seductive wink, I realize she wasn't talking to me.

"They definitely have an effect on me," he whispers before nipping at her throat.

She laughs, and my dad clears his throat.

"Sorry," Dustin apologizes to me.

"For what?" I ask, pressing the issue. These people still see me as a child, and it grates on my nerves.

"Kid shouldn't behave like that around you," my dad mumbles.

"Shouldn't act like he's in love?" I counter.

"You know what I mean."

"I know that Landon is the only child in this clubhouse other than baby Amelia, and he's probably already back in his room playing video games," I argue. "Stop treating me like a baby who doesn't know what sex is or what foreplay looks like."

"Jasmine," my mom chastises.

"No," I hiss, holding up my hand to silence her. "I'm thirty, Dad. I know what sex is. I have sex."

His jaw tenses, and he refuses to pull his eyes from his plate on the table in front of him. Mom was the one responsible for the sex talk. Dad tried, but his only advice years ago was a long conversation about how boys are dogs and sex is just something I shouldn't do until I'm thirty. Well, I'm there, and it seems he still has a problem with it.

"I like sex. So, no, Dustin doesn't have to stop teasing his wife because you think it makes me uncomfortable. It doesn't. I'm happy for them. You should be, too."

"I'm happy for them," he argues. "I just didn't want—"

"You have to stop seeing a child when you look at me."

His eyes find mine, and suddenly I feel like a complete jerk for having this little fit in front of my dad's friends. It isn't until Kincaid chuckles that I look down to see not only him but also Shadow, Misty, and Emmalyn watching me with a smile.

Before my dad can say anything else, I excuse myself from the table and walk out of the room. This is not the way I saw this day going. Never once have I considered speaking to my dad that way. It may not seem like a big deal, but for the most part, I always just went along with his expectations.

There's only one situation I want to be in right now, and it surely isn't looking in the bathroom mirror begging myself not to cry.

Chapter 20

Max

"Where do you think she went?" I ask Kingston as he leads us into his room.

"No clue."

We both saw Jasmine having a heated conversation with her dad before she stormed out of the room. Unease settled around the Cerberus guys and one by one they all made their excuses and left the family and friends together to continue celebrating the newly married couple.

"Should we go look for her?"

"No," Kingston answers.

"Then what should we do?"

He rakes his hands over the top of his head. "I don't fucking know."

I leave him to his pacing, opting to sit on his bed rather than waste my own energy. I learned so much during the meeting with Cerberus today, and I know even as I sit here idle, things are being done to bring my sister home. They have a good idea where she's being kept but moving right this minute isn't an option. As an agent, I understand that. Going in blind would be a suicide mission, and that doesn't help anyone involved.

As a brother, I feel helpless and hopeless, just waiting for things to fall into place. Every minute Mia spends with those cartel assholes is another opportunity for them to hurt her. I can't even think of the other options. Her not being there when Cerberus raids the Jiménez compound isn't something I'll consider.

Before I can open my mouth to offer other ways to release tension than pacing, a soft knock hits the bedroom door.

Kingston sighs heavily before walking across the room and opening the door. Jasmine stands on the other side, a small smile on her pretty lips. She's just the distraction we both need.

"You shouldn't be here," Kingston hisses, and anger fills my blood when her face falls with the declaration.

"Don't be an asshole," I mutter as I stand from the bed and shove him out of the way.

Jasmine takes my hand the second I offer it to her.

"You're just asking for trouble," Kingston says as I close the door behind her. "Dominic and Kincaid will kill us both if they catch you in here."

"They're busy celebrating," Jasmine reminds him.

I want to wrap my arms around her, sink my nose into the soft skin of her neck, but I'm not the one driving this situation. She is, and Jasmine seems just as happy to stand in the middle of the room in a dress that, although it looks amazing on her, would look even better in a puddle on the floor.

"What can I say," she begins with her eyes on the grumpy man, "I'm a risk-taker."

"Yet, it's not your life you're taking a risk with."

"I'm a grown woman," she argues. "My dad has no say over what I do."

"Even when it's with two men, under his brother's roof?"

"Who said anything about two men?" Jasmine's cheeks pink when she makes the declaration, but she turns to me, anyway.

Her arms wrap around my neck as she pulls me closer.

"You're poking an angry bear," I mutter against her lips.

"Do you want me to leave?" She doesn't pull away when she asks. If anything, she steps a little closer.

The satin of her dress brushes my forearms, and I'm having second thoughts about wanting it on the floor. Up against my naked body while she undulates on me is sounding better by the second.

I fist the fabric at her ass and pull her against me, effectively removing every inch of distance between us.

"We started something back in my apartment earlier that I'd like to finish."

Her words come out on a moan as my teeth nip at the valley of her neck. Her pulse pounds, and it only serves to escalate my own.

Agitated that he knows he's going to end up joining in, Kingston continues to pace the length of his room.

"He's going to wear a hole in the carpet if you don't acknowledge him soon," I tell her.

"He's a grown man. I told him before that he has to take what he wants. I'm not going to treat him with kid gloves."

"You also didn't offer an invitation."

"Are you complaining? Wouldn't want me all to yourself?"

I contemplate that for a second. Jasmine is an amazing woman, everything most men could want, but I'm not most men.

"This doesn't work without him."

Her eyes search mine as if she's looking for understanding. I'll back away from her now if she doesn't feel the same way. I like Jasmine, she's amazing, but Kingston, no matter how much distance is between us, has always been the love of my life.

"You're right," she says, planting a soft kiss on my lips. "But he's still going to have to come to me. I don't chase after any man."

"So, he needs to take it?"

"Exactly."

We're talking loud enough for him to hear, but not once have his steps faltered.

"Take," I say again, and she nods her head.

Only now do his feet stutter on the carpet. My eyes find his over her shoulder, and I see the second he makes his decision. I don't warn her, and even though I know it's coming, my cock still jerks in my borrowed dress slacks when he grips the messy knot of hair at her nape.

"You want to be taken, Jasmine?"

A breathy whimper is her only response.

"Hike your dress up. I need to see what you've been hiding all evening under that silky fabric."

My fingers itch to obey his command even though he isn't talking to me.

She doesn't hesitate, but the trembling in her hands complicate her ability to shift the fabric on the first try. I step back, watching with heated eyes as her legs are revealed. Next is the apex at her thighs. The lacy fabric of her panties has to be wet, but that's something we'll find out shortly. This is Kingston's show, and I'm not one to interfere. We're both benefiting from her little performance.

Without thought, my hand grips my thickness. I hate the layers that separate my skin from that of my cock, but all in due time.

"Do you want me to fuck you?"

With her hands holding the fabric up around her waist, Kingston presses to her back. The biting clamp of his fingers on her throat makes my own breathing hitch. As if unable to speak, she merely nods her head. Mine mimics the action. Somehow, he's speaking to both of us.

"You're going to learn, pretty girl, that you don't always get what you want." Kingston's words are a growl, and the sound makes me remember the way he used to approach me.

When we first took things a little further than longing glances, he'd get pissed. The bias and evil from his father had no other option but to bleed over into his own thoughts and actions. He was attracted to me. He knew that he needed things from me that weren't what he would consider normal, and he hated himself for it. Aggression was how he managed to overcome that hate, and it spilled into more than one session we'd had as teens. Jasmine is topping from the bottom, and he doesn't know how to handle that other than taking back his control.

Enjoying the show, I rush to tug my cock free from my pants.

"Is your pussy wet?"

"Dr-drenched," she answers, and as if her words have magic, her scent blooms around the room, filling it with the humid dampness of desire and the promise of things to come.

"Well, guess what isn't wet?" I'm all ears because this conversation is almost enough to send me over the edge. "Max's cock isn't wet. You need to remedy that for him."

Before she can agree, Kingston is applying pressure on her shoulders and forcing her to her knees.

Force isn't the right words because she doesn't fall, rather one hand presses on her while the other guides her. He's still in power, still playing both of us like a master puppeteer.

As if he's pulled my own strings, I step closer, not wasting a second before pushing my dick past her painted pink lips. We both moan at the same time.

"Don't drop your dress," he warns as she releases the fabric to wrap her hands around my cock. When she holds me in her mouth, focusing on regathering the dress, I twitch with exhilaration. I'm wondering how long it will take me to get hard again if I come suddenly when he speaks again. "Keep still. You aren't giving him your mouth; he's *taking* it."

"Jesus," I hiss, but take his command as gospel.

My hips push forward, slowly at first before increasing the tempo.

"Is that how you'd fuck her cunt?" Kingston asks disapprovingly.

"God, yes." It's the truth. Not everything has to be a race to the finish line.

Pushing on my arm, Kingston shoves me away as he drops his own zipper and pulls his dick out. "She wants to be taken. So, you need to give the woman what she wants."

He rams her mouth full of his cock, but her deep moans aren't ones of discomfort. He's giving her exactly what she wants.

"If she isn't choking on it, she isn't happy." He thrusts several more times, and not once do her hands even move to push him away. "See how her thighs tremble? I bet her pussy is leaking down her legs. Cry for me, baby."

We both watch as moisture pools on her lower lashes before running down her face in black streaks from her makeup.

"So fucking pretty," Kingston purrs as he reaches down and smears the tears more.

Her face is a mess. Her lips ringed with lipstick as he plows in and out of her. She keeps her eyes pointed up at him as her moans around his dick speak of her own need, but I don't reach for her. He hasn't given us permission yet.

"You want me to come?" He sounds like he's on edge already. "Not yet."

He rips from her mouth, turning her head to take my own cock back down her throat.

"She doesn't like gentle," Kingston reminds me when I slide in on a slow glide.

I'm seconds away from arguing with him, reminding him that her mouth is on me, and I'll take it how I see fit, but then I realize that this is about her and her needs, not mine.

My hands reach up, fisting both sides of her head as I flex my hips and slam back into her mouth. Where were the girls with no gag reflexes in the last decade? A man could fall in love with a woman able to swallow around the head of his cock and not choke.

"That's it," Kingston praises, one hand on my ass urging it forward with each thrust and the other cupping her cheek while I fuck into her mouth. "So pretty."

"...is landing!" I hear from the hallway but ignore the intrusion, seconds away from coming.

"What the fuck?" Kingston asks as we hear it again.

But it's too late. Her mouth is just too good. The door bursts open the second my cock jerks with release.

"What the hell is going on?!"

I'm a dead man, I realize when I see Dominic standing in the open doorway of Kingston's bedroom. Even the sight of him doesn't stop the train already moving. My cum shoots Jasmine on the cheek when she turns her head toward her father and again on her neck when she struggles to stand.

"Dad! Get out!" Jasmine screams, but Dominic stands there with fire in his eyes.

Chapter 21

Tug

"He'll be fine," Jasmine says, but the tremble in her voice betrays the lie.

Thankfully, Dominic pulled the door closed, but I can still feel his fury on the other side of the wall.

"He saw us with both our dicks out," I remind her through gritted teeth. "A dad won't ever be fine with walking in on that."

"Do you think they'll refuse to find Mia now?" These are the first words Max has spoken since we were busted in on.

At first, I want to punch him in the nose for being so fucking selfish, but when I give myself a second to calm down and put myself in his position, I know getting Mia back is the priority. God help me if I fucked this up for him by not being able to resist the goddess in a silky dress.

"He wouldn't do that," Jasmine says as she cups his jaw, forcing him to look down at her.

"It's really hard to take you seriously right now," he mutters.

"Because I'm a woman?" she snaps.

"Because you have cum drying on your face."

He can't take her seriously, and I just want to lick it off for her.

I smack the front of my forehead with my hand, but even after everything that's happened and the possibility of facing a war outside this door, I still haven't gotten to sink inside of her yet, and my balls are all too ready to remind me of that fact.

"Washroom," I grunt and point across the room to the door beside the closet. "Get cleaned up. It's on your shoulder and neck as well."

"What do we do now?" Max asks, but I don't have answers for him.

Until we face what we've done, I won't be able to tell him a thing. Just the thought of stepping out of this room makes my hands shake with nerves.

"He won't understand," I mutter.

What I don't say is that I may lose my job, and as many jobs as I could find with my skill set, Cerberus has become home to me. It's not just about work. It's the camaraderie and the brotherhood that embraced me the second I stepped foot on this land. Now, I've fucked it up because I was unable to keep my dick in my pants.

"Isn't another Cerberus dude with Kincaid's daughter?"

I whispered all the connections in the clubhouse to Max while we waited for the ceremony to start. He got a little tangled up on the fact that Delilah was technically marrying her stepbrother, but it seems he was paying attention to everything I said, classic Max, hanging on my every word.

"That's a little different than two guys making your daughter choke on their dicks." We both heard the commotion out in the hallway, but he walked into this room before either of us could put our dicks away. It was evident by our proximity exactly what was going on, and the fact that Max sprayed her with jizz while he watched was just one more nail in our coffins.

"Well," Max says with a slap on my back, "I've already died once. What's another time?"

"No one is dying," Jasmine says as she walks out of my bathroom rubbing a hand towel over her face.

I miss the smeared ring of lipstick and streaks of mascara down her face immediately. She's pretty on any given day but seeing the aftermath of what we could do to her will live in my dreams forever.

For a split second, I was willing to tell Dominic that I'd back off, that I'd never put my filthy hands on her again, but then I realized those would only be lies. There isn't a chance in hell I can keep my filthy paws off of her. Hell, even facing a firing squad, I'm still seconds away from reaching for her and finishing what we've started several times now and haven't had the chance to finish.

"Keep looking at me like that," she warns.

"And what?" I ask, turning in her direction and stalking closer to her.

"Hello?" Max snaps. "We don't have time for that shit."

Jasmine pouts, and my cock begs me to disagree with him.

"You're right," she says in Max's direction before looking back at me. "Rain check?"

"You're willing to consider it? Even after your dad beats us to a pulp?"

"What can he do?" she asks with a shoulder shrug that's easy for her, seeing as she isn't the one about to walk into hell. "I'm a grown woman."

"We need to talk to him alone."

"Not a chance," she says.

"I don't like that idea at all," Max says at the same time.

I narrow my eyes at him. He was always the one to want to take the easy way out. He'd rather sweep things under the rug than face them like a man. Trying to use Jasmine as a buffer between her dad and us is just another way to avoid responsibility.

"When I leave this clubhouse tonight, it will be with all three of us heading to my apartment."

"Perfect plan," Max says, and now he's the one closing the distance between the two of them.

"Why do you want to poke the hornet's nest?" I ask, glowering at Max for touching her when he just got onto us for getting close to doing the very same thing.

"Quit acting like babies," Jasmine says as she sidesteps Max and makes her way to the bedroom door. "Man up and let's go."

"Man up," I grumble as I follow her out the door.

Max, of course, stays a few steps behind like I knew he would.

As if she already knew what was going on, Jasmine opens the door to the meeting room, and we follow her in.

Expecting to only see Dominic in here, I'm shocked when I notice Kincaid, his wife, and Jasmine's mom as well.

"Is this really necessary?" Jasmine asks in a huff as we enter the room and close the door.

"I want an explanation," Dominic demands instead of answering her.

"I don't owe you an explanation," Jasmine snaps.

"We—" I begin, but Jasmine spins and presses her hand to my lips.

"Hush," she hisses.

One of the other women chuckles, but I keep my eyes on Jasmine, so I don't know who it was.

"Let him speak," Dominic urges. "I'm curious how he'll explain taking advantage of my daughter."

"I don't think that's what's going on," Kincaid mutters.

"Why are you even in here?" Dominic snaps at his brother.

"To make sure you don't kill them," my boss answers, simply.

"That still hasn't been decided." The growl of Dominic's voice assures me that even with Kincaid in here, the man has the ability to act on his anger. Murder may not be the outcome, but serious bodily injury is definitely a possibility.

"Mom?" Jasmine looks at Makayla for help. "Tell him I'm grown and can do whatever I like."

"I agree with you, Jasmine, but acting out this way at Delilah's wedding because you're angry at your dad isn't the right way to handle things. *Grown* women don't do things that are petty and vindictive."

"It wasn't... that's not why... this didn't just start tonight. I didn't seek them out as some form of revenge because Dad can't stop reminding me that he thinks I'm a child."

Dominic's glare only intensifies. "How long has it been going on?"

Oh, fuck.

If she mentions the club, we're sure as hell gonna meet our maker tonight.

"Weeks," I tell him with my back straight. I don't have any intentions of lying to the man but giving him every single detail isn't going to happen either. Even though we started this as a means to have a little fun in Denver, we're way past that now. This is no longer just a way to get my rocks off. I don't know exactly where it's heading, but somehow Jasmine and Max together is everything I never let myself hope for. Fuck him if he thinks I'm going to give it up.

"And just today you decide to bring him here to get help with his sister?" Dominic sneers. "You'd think you'd have better priorities than spending weeks fucking my daughter rather than getting help for a woman you told Cerberus was as close as a sister for you."

"I haven't fucked your daughter," I growl.

At this point, it's merely semantics, but if he wants the truth, he'll fucking get it.

"This situation is complicated. Jasmine and I didn't know about Mia's abduction until last night."

"We should go back out to the party," Emmalyn says as she clasps Kincaid's elbow.

He doesn't move, and I know he won't leave his brother until he calms down. From the look in Dominic's eyes, that's not going to happen any time soon.

"Daddy, you have to let me live my life," Jasmine says as she steps between him and me.

"I won't let men take advantage of you." Surprisingly, his words no longer hold the anger they did moments ago.

"They aren't. I promise."

"It's highly unusual," Kincaid adds.

"You can't compare your situation to every other one to make it fit. People are different. Isn't that what you guys raised me to believe?" Jasmine moves her head, looking between her father and her uncle. "If people are happy and not hurting others, then it's none of our business how they live?"

"Are you telling me you're in a committed relationship with two men?" Dominic challenges. "That was the point of those conversations, baby girl. If it makes someone happy, then it's okay."

"I'm happy," she says, effectively avoiding the other question.

"And you two are fine with—"

"That's enough, Daddy. Leave them alone," Jasmine interrupts.

For once, I'm a little frustrated with her. I wanted him to ask. I wanted to face these men I respect and tell them that I was with both of them, but I honestly have no idea where I stand with either one. Other than what I expect to be a fulfilling sexual encounter, I have no idea where we'll end up after that.

Dominic stands first, and although he doesn't shake my hand, he nods at me briefly before walking out of the room. Kincaid does the same, and everyone is gone before I have the chance to ask if I need to pack my shit and leave. Without a word to either Max or Jasmine, I turn and leave the room. I'll gather my shit before they have the chance to tell me to do so.

How this day went from the magic of sinking a few inches into Jasmine's tight cunt to falling down around me, I'll never know.

Chapter 22

Jasmine

"Are you sure you don't need to stay?" Max asks from the passenger seat as Kingston throws his duffel bag in the back of the SUV.

"I spent the day with the girls. Delilah will understand," I answer, "as soon as I get the chance to explain things to her."

"And exactly how will that explanation go?" Kingston asks as he slides his ass into the driver's seat.

"Easily, I imagine." I don't answer the real question he's asking, simply because I don't know the real answer.

I can't make assumptions about what this is between the three of us because I don't know. It's also a series of questions that are too serious for right now. Maybe after we get Mia back and everyone can step back and take a breath, but right now, I'm not going to risk making declarations or talking about what I'm feeling when I don't think either of the guys are on the same page. Not that I know definitively what page I'm on. This is just as new to me, and I still feel like a third wheel and interloper on whatever has been left unsaid between the two of them. The real outcome of all of this is probably going to be Max and King together with me on the outside. And since that makes my heart hurt a little just thinking about it, I want to put that conversation off as long as I can.

"It'll be an easy conversation?" Kingston asks, his eyes finding mine in the rearview as he pulls out onto the road leaving the clubhouse behind us.

"I'm just saying she'll understand once she has the details why I didn't stay as long as everyone expected me to at the reception."

He doesn't answer, and all the way back to my apartment, Max doesn't fill the empty silence. We're all stuck in our heads, waiting for something none of us can anticipate.

The sexual energy that filled the room even after my dad backed out of the bedroom door is gone now. Only exhaustion and a million unanswered questions remain. Max climbs out of the truck the second Kingston puts it in park, but I stay in the back seat just watching the side of his face for any sign that he has things figured out more than the rest of us. When his eyes close and his fingers pinch the bridge of his nose, I have my answer. He's just as clueless.

"Did you lie to your dad when you told him you were happy?"

His question strikes a chord, but even as frustrating as it is, I still don't have a good answer.

"Are you asking if I was happy on my knees choking on both of your cocks?"

There isn't a hint of innuendo or suggestion in my voice. I'm not asking because I want to steer us right back to that moment. I'm not trying to distract him from the bigger issues none of us seem to want to talk about. More than anything, I want to know if there is more to this than just sexual acts. I don't think the answer would change the direction of where we're heading, but the momentum may alter a little.

"I already know you were happy on your knees, Jasmine. Delight shined in your eyes with every fucking thrust."

Max is sitting on the small concrete bench near the entrance to the elevator, but he isn't glaring at us for having this moment, rather he's allowing it.

The dried-up sexual energy hits me again full force, and if I were younger, I'd attempt to climb over the back of the seat to straddle his lap.

"Answer me."

The snap of his voice and the command makes me question my own submissiveness. I so easily shoved it down at the club, so sure that I didn't have an ounce of it in my body, but he seems to bring it out of me.

"Be more specific. What exactly do you want to know?"

"Are you happy with this? With us?" When I meet his imploring eyes, I can tell what answer he wants me to give, and just the thought of offering that to him makes my blood sing.

"Could I be happy with two men?" He nods. "I think so, yes."

"You think?"

"Is this a decision I need to make today?"

His jaw flexes, the tension from clenching his teeth making the muscles more pronounced.

"Listen, I'm not being flippant about this, but this is new to me. You two may have done this before, but I've never been a third."

"We haven't—we don't—this isn't like a thing we do. When Max and I were together when we were younger, it was just us. We lost, well *I* lost, my virginity to him. It was always only him."

"And I'm getting in the way of that." Tears burn the backs of my eyes. As much as I wanted to avoid this damn conversation, here we are having it anyway.

He turns his head so he can watch Max out the windshield. "You aren't a third. You're part of three."

I don't bother arguing basic math to him. I get the sentiment he's trying to get across.

"So, you're saying we're a triad?"

I've heard the word used more than once, but I always figured someone was eventually left off. Two of the people would end up loving each other more than the third person. As much as I want to be an equal partner in whatever this is going on between us, I still can't wrap my head around three people being complete. My only frame of reference is two people, be it a man and a woman or two men. Things didn't work out with Jaxon, Rob, and Lawson's mom. Even though they started out that way, according to my eavesdropping several years ago when Lawson and his brother Drew showed up out of the blue on the Cerberus doorstep.

"I don't know what I'm saying." His hands are rough as they scrape over the top of his head, and it kind of makes me happy that he's just as frustrated as me.

If he's thinking about what all of this could mean, then he's not just sitting there assuming we're just going to mess around a couple of times then walk away. His questions mean he's at least a little interested in wondering where we will all end up when the dust settles.

"Do we have to decide all of this tonight?"

He shakes his head. "I don't think this could possibly be decided tonight."

We both watch Max, who, although he doesn't look agitated to be on the outside right now, watches us from the bench. I can't say I'd be as calm if I were the one sitting on the outside, but those are my issues to deal with, not theirs.

"What happens when we get inside?" I ask because I seriously just need to know where my head needs to be.

"What do you want to happen?"

"Are you saying I'm the one who gets to decide?" A teasing smile plays at my lips, but his eyes are still locked on the man he thought was dead for the last decade.

"You'll never be in charge, Jasmine. That's something you'll have to learn to deal with." Pulling his eyes from Max, he turns his head slightly, so he can see me in his periphery. "But tonight, you get to determine the outcome."

"I'm exhausted," I confess.

"So, we'll sleep. Come on."

He slides out of the SUV and pulls open the back door for me. I wait beside the vehicle as he grabs his things from the back and we walk toward Max with his hand low on my back.

"I'm beat," Max says as he stands, arms stretching over his head in exaggerated fatigue. "I hope you two didn't have plans for my body tonight. If so, just know I'm going to lie there like a dead fish."

"I'm tired, too," I confess as he sidles up to my other side as we climb onto the waiting elevator.

"I need to shower," Kingston grumbles as he hits the button for my floor.

"Now that's a plan I can get behind," Max says as he muffles a yawn.

Maybe he isn't as tired as he professed. I thought there was a conversation they had between the two of them like the guys back at the clubhouse did all the time, but maybe not.

The sexual hum tingles around us when we make our way inside my apartment, but no one makes any overtures. We take turns taking showers, Max and I conceding to let Kingston go first since he spoke the words before either of us. When I get out of my shower, I fully expect to find them on the bed much the same way I did this morning, but they are just chatting. I climb into bed, too tired to argue about where everyone is sleeping. I'd be a fool to even try, so it's no surprise when Kingston climbs into the bed with me. We both laugh when we hear Max singing at the top of his lungs.

"He's crazy," Kingston mutters as he pulls me against his chest.

I don't argue or fight him on it. Honestly, it's right where I need to be, but then a little guilt settles in my stomach. I slept on him last night, so shouldn't Max get a turn?

My head is still running over this issue when Max walks in butt-assed naked, drying his hair with a towel. He isn't fully aroused, but his cock isn't completely limp either.

"You two look amazing together," Max says without an ounce of jealousy in his voice. "But you're missing one thing."

"What's that?" Kingston asks, and the hum of his chest under my cheek is soothing.

"Me. Scoot over."

With my eyes closed, I inch even closer to Kingston, so sure I left plenty of room behind me.

"The other way sweetheart," Kingston says.

When I lift my head to look at him, my throat closes. This whole time I was worried about the guys getting upset about having to share me, but with Max climbing in on Kingston's side, they're making it very clear. I'm not the one being shared, Kingston is.

"Yeah," I say, my voice seconds away from cracking. "Sure."

"Not that far," Max says as he reaches for me.

I'm already on the other side of the bed, willing to give them their space.

"Come here." Max waves me over with a slow crook of his fingers.

Once again, he pulls me to Kingston's side, just as the man in question wraps his arm around my back to make sure there isn't an inch of room between us. Max turns off the lamp on that side of the bed, and then I feel him settle on Kingston's other side. When my eyes adjust to the darkness, I find Max's eyes on mine and Kingston's eyes closed with a look of contentment I've never seen on his lips.

"Night, sweetheart," Max says softly before angling his head to press his lips to mine.

The kiss is soft, filled with the promise of what could happen while at the same time letting me know tonight's not going to be that night. After pulling away, Max lifts his body on his elbow and lowers his mouth to Kingston's.

"Night, King," he whispers against his lips.

My own tingle with disappointment. It isn't lost on me that Kingston still has never kissed me. Even though I'm on his chest with his arm wrapped tightly around me, I'll fall asleep once again without knowing what his lips taste like.

He told me in the vehicle only an hour ago that I wasn't a third but part of a three, but it hits home just how full of shit he was. Part of three meant equals, sharing everything, matching behaviors with everyone. I still haven't been kissed, and from the conversations the guys have had, I've deduced that Max has never had the opportunity to slide his cock anywhere other than Kingston's mouth. So, Max and I are both left without equal parts. Seems like the king always gets what he wants while leaving everyone else without.

Chapter 23

Max

"Can't we just turn off the sun?" I grumble against Kingston's chest when the light from the open blinds hit me directly in my scrunched-up eyes.

"Shhh," Kingston says. "Look."

I follow the tip of his finger to see Jasmine curled up in a ball as far away from the two of us as possible without hitting the floor.

"Think she's used to sleeping alone?" I ask.

"I'm used to sleeping alone," Kingston growls. I love his damn growl. It's possessive and full of jealousy. "You don't see me trying to get away from either of you."

"Hey," I slap at his chest, "I always sleep alone, too."

I don't know if he was trying to imply that I have people in my bed often, but honestly, how would he even know. I've been dead for the last ten years.

"I think she's upset," I tell him when I give myself the chance to think a little longer on it. "She moved away last night when I climbed in. The heartbreak in her eyes nearly gutted me."

"She's awake and doesn't like to be talked about like she isn't here," Jasmine says, climbing off the bed and leaving the room without a backward glance.

Both of us are off the bed and following after her, but she makes it to the bathroom and locks the door before we can stop her. I turn and head toward the coffee pot, but Kingston leans his head against the door for a long moment before joining me in the kitchen.

"Those aren't the actions of a man who's only interested in getting off," I chide him when he enters the room.

"What the fuck are you talking about?"

He doesn't face me; instead, he pulls three cups from the cabinet and places them beside the coffee pot before turning back to open the fridge.

"Yesterday morning I told you that you have feelings for her. You assured me that you're here because she gets your dick hard."

"I never said I didn't have feelings for her," he argues.

"And even now you aren't."

"Are you jealous, Vazquez?"

"I don't have any reason to be," I tell him, simply.

"So fucking sure of yourself," he spits, vitriol lacing his tone as he turns toward me. "You seriously think that because you're here now that there isn't another person on this earth that could compete with you? You think you've got me wrapped around your finger? Like all you have to do is let a little smile cross those perfect fucking lips of yours and I'll come running like some fucking lap dog that's eager to be petted by his owner?"

My head snaps back. That's a lot of fucking anger for so damn early in the morning.

"Are you done?"

"Yeah." His eyes look me up and down as disgust mars his handsome face. "I'm fucking done."

I grab him by the arm before he can head back to the room. I've seen this before. This is how he acted whenever I questioned his feelings for me in the beginning. He didn't know what to do with them, so he took them out on me. His father was famous for using his fists, and even though that wasn't Kingston's style, he never shied away from spitting venom like it was second nature.

He stops but refuses to turn back and face me. He has ten years and a lifetime of anger at me on his shoulders now, but letting him walk away, letting him go to the room to get dressed so he can storm away like he has always done in the past, isn't going to happen. We are no longer teens who didn't have complete control over our lives. We can no longer blame others for our choices. As grown men, we have to face our own realities, make our own choices, and then live with the fucking consequences. I'll be damned if he walks away from me again.

"I don't have to be jealous of her," I hiss in his ear. His body stiffens again. "I want her as much as you do, as much as you want me. This isn't about her or me individually. I'm not snapping my fingers to get you to fall in line or using our history to manipulate you. I don't want you wrapped around my finger. I don't see the fun in that at all. It isn't my nature. I'd love to have you wrapped around my cock, but I gave you my power in the bed thirteen years ago. I don't want it back."

I don't have to look over his shoulder to know his cock is standing at attention in his boxers. The thought makes me realize I'm still naked from my shower.

"Now go wait outside of the bathroom door for our girl. I'm going to borrow some of your clothes and get dressed."

I press my lips to his cheek and scurry past him. Even though she took a shower last night, I hear the water turn off as I walk past the bathroom. I already know what we're going to find when she finally walks out of there.

Sure enough, when I get back in the kitchen to pour a cup of coffee, Jasmine is standing against the counter with her own cup close to her lips. Her eyes are rimmed red, and even though the shower hid her tears from herself, the evidence of them is still on her face.

Forgetting about my own need for coffee, I walk right up to her and wrap my arms around her waist.

"Good morning, sweetheart." She stiffens when I press my lips to hers.

"If you don't want me to kiss you, just tell me," I whisper.

"I don't want you to touch me," she clarifies.

I back away immediately, but don't bother to hide the surprise on my face. My eyes dart to Kingston, who looks just as growly as I've ever seen him.

"What did you say to her?" I snap in his direction.

"Nothing," he mutters.

"Bullshit," I argue. "Had to have been something. I was only gone for a few minutes."

Jasmine sets her coffee down on the counter and tries to walk past me. She isn't walking away from me today either. What has gotten into these two?

"Tell me what he did, sweetheart, and I'll make it all better." I add a playfulness to my voice, hoping that maybe she just isn't a morning person.

Maybe I hogged the covers last night. Maybe one of us snores or farts in our sleep. Women are weird, so it could be something simple.

"Don't do that," Kingston hisses. "Don't fucking team up against me. That isn't how this is going to work."

"This?" Jasmine glares at him. "What exactly is *this*?"

I don't have an answer, so I look at Kingston, hoping he does. If anything, he's the one who should know.

Looking dumbfounded, Kingston lowers his eyes to his own cup of coffee.

"No answer?" she presses. "You had all the answers last night. Do you need a few minutes to think of some more lies?"

"I haven't lied to you." Each word leaves his lips with increasing agitation.

"What did you two talk about?" I hate being in the dark, especially when it has something to do with things that affect my own life. I knew I shouldn't have left them alone for so long in the truck.

"I'm not having that conversation again," Jasmine says with a sigh that makes it clear she's already tired from what little we have spoken today.

"Maybe we should," Kingston says, stepping in her way before she can dart out of the kitchen. "Because it seems like we're not on the same page, which I was certain we were last night."

"I thought about what we talked about and decided that I don't want to be a part of three or a third or have anything to do with whatever you decide I should be satisfied with getting. It's not enough. It'll never be enough."

Her words sting as she shoves past Kingston, and I feel like it was aimed more at me than at him. She wants him to herself, and I'm in the way of that. They both said nothing had happened between them before that first night we all hooked up in the glass room back at the club in Denver, but that doesn't mean they were honest. There could have been feelings or glances over group dinners. Maybe a little flirting by the pool I saw behind the clubhouse yesterday. Maybe something was building between the two of them, and neither of them was aware of it until they discovered who the other was and how they were both connected to the club. Hell, they teamed up to abduct and interrogate me. That's proof they're more connected than they let on.

With resolve, I nod my head and walk past Kingston.

"And just where the fuck do you think you're going?"

"I know when I'm not wanted." Sadness fills his eyes as I slip my arms into my jacket. "You have my number, let me know when they're getting ready to move on Jimenez. I want to be there when they pull my sister from that hellhole."

"You didn't want me to leave earlier, but now you think it's okay for you to walk out on me?" He points down the hall. "On us?"

"Thirteen years ago, I begged harder than you are now," I remind him, "and you still walked out on me."

With my final words, I leave the apartment. My eyes stay on her door the entire time I wait for the elevator. He never walks out to ask me to stay.

Chapter 24

Tug

My hands flex, itching to punch a hole in the wall, but this isn't my place. Hell, I wouldn't punch a hole in the wall at Cerberus either. That fact leaves me with more anger and tension in my body than I know what to do with.

Following after Max was my first instinct, but I've known the man for years, and he needs a little time to calm down.

I know when I'm not wanted.

His words don't make any fucking sense. What part of holding the man against me all night screamed that he wasn't wanted. As sexy as the jealous streak was in high school, it has no place in our adult lives. Only moments before his little shit fit, he told me he wanted Jasmine as much as I did. I thought we were all finally on the same page. Now they're both upset.

My eyes hit the front door before shifting to the closed bedroom door. Solving the problem closest to me seems like the best idea, so I make my way down the hall.

I stop short of throwing open the door and demanding she get over whatever is causing her attitude problem, but I imagine that will go over like a lead balloon.

With gentle knuckles, I tap my hand on her door. There isn't a response, not one sound coming from her room. It's petty and immature for both of them to be acting this way. I'll remind them that this is why I always have to take control.

"Jasmine?"

I tap on the door again, but before I can raise my voice and insist that she speak with me, my phone buzzes on the kitchen counter.

"Fuck," I grunt as I make my way to retrieve it.

It's not a text from Max apologizing for acting like a child, but a text from Shadow. Things are moving a lot quicker than I expected.

Without another thought, I head straight for the bedroom. I was giving her space before, but my clothes are in there, and I have fifteen minutes to get back to the clubhouse.

"Babe?" Confusion draws my brow in when I walk in the room to find it empty. "Jasmine?"

Irritation grows exponentially when I pull her closet door open to find her standing in her bra and panties, looking at her clothes. I'm not annoyed at the sight of her creamy skin, but the fact that I called for her twice, and she ignored me.

"We'll talk about this when I get back," I assure her as I shove my legs into a pair of jeans.

She doesn't acknowledge me.

"Both you and Max are the most immature adults I've ever met," I mutter as I finish getting dressed. "Jasmine?"

Only now does she turn to face me with a blank expression on her face.

"We all need to sit down and talk. We need to be on the same page. This guessing what's going on or trying to predict expectations without all the facts isn't going to work."

"I want my key back."

She finally speaks, and that's the bullshit she wants to go with.

"Not a chance," I tell her before walking out of her room.

Hating to leave her, but having no other choice, I climb in the SUV and speed all the way back to the clubhouse.

Facing Dominic won't be fun, and if I'm being honest, I'm surprised I haven't been sent separation papers from Kincaid. I was hoping to stay away longer than fourteen hours – give Jasmine's family time to come to terms with what we have going on – but the Mia situation takes precedence.

"There's the ballsy bastard," Scooter says the second I walk through the front door.

Several of the guys are working to reverse the winter wonderland from yesterday.

"Shut up," I mutter, walking past him.

He catches me with an arm around my shoulder before I can get far.

"Figured you wouldn't show your face around here after pissing off Poppa Bear," he taunts.

"Leave him the fuck alone," Rocker says as he approaches. "Dominic isn't happy, but he's not going stand in the way of true love."

"It's not—"

Brazenly, Rocker presses his hand to my mouth. "Don't say that's not what it is because the only way you may survive his wrath is by making a declaration."

I'll be damned. I'm not saying something to a man I respect when I haven't even thought of Jasmine in those terms. I'm not saying we won't ever get there. I'm not saying that I only see her as a good time. But declaring anything this early is incredibly premature.

"Do we have a meeting or what?" I hiss when Rocker pulls his hand away from my mouth. I wipe my face on the back of my arm and scowl at him.

A knock on the front door grabs all of our attention.

"That has to be Max," I tell them as I turn to grab the door.

I texted him as I was walking down the stairs in Jasmine's apartment complex. He didn't respond, but I knew he wouldn't be far behind me. No matter how pissed he is at me, he won't let that anger come between him and finding his sister. I'd never allow it, either.

He doesn't say a word or bother to make true eye contact with me when I open the door. He nods at Rocker and Scooter as he steps past me and follows Rocker into the meeting room.

"Trouble in paradise?" Scooter asks as I hang my head and walk in the same direction.

"Shut the fuck up."

Unlike the last time we met with Cerberus, I leave Max standing to the side and take my usual seat at the table. If he wants to be petty like Jasmine, then I can do the same.

Now knowing what they're dealing with, the guys don't seem as anxious as we wait for Kincaid to speak. They chat with each other about the party last night and how several of them ended up at *Jake's*. They talk of plans for the holidays since Christmas is literally five days away. Some are heading out soon to visit with family, others without families are bragging about plans with various women.

"We were unable to confirm that Mia Vazquez is inside Jiménez's Florida compound," Kincaid says the second he walks into the room.

My eyes immediately bolt to Max. He looks crestfallen. He broke the last time we were here, but this time it's going to be ten times worse. This time he had hope, had the support of Cerberus in bringing home his sister.

I'm raising from my seat to go to my oldest friend when Kincaid raises his hand.

"We don't have proof that she isn't there either," he adds.

"So, we're going fishing?" Scooter asks with glee.

"Get your gear ready," Shadow says from the corner. "Wheels up in an hour."

"What's going on?" Max asks anyone who's listening as the guys crowd out of the room.

"We're going to Florida to look for your sister," Rocker tells him with a brotherly slap on the back.

As much as I want to go to Max, I also have to get ready to leave.

"Tug," Kincaid calls when I turn to walk out of the room, "a word?"

"Sir?" I say when I turn back around.

With my head held high, I face him. He's going to fire me. I just know it. I'd argue that starting things with Jasmine was worth it, but I'm not certain where we even stand right now.

"You can't join the guys for the infiltration into the compound."

"Like hel—"

"This isn't a punishment," Dominic says as he stands from the table and crosses the room to stand beside his brother.

"It sure as hell feels like it."

"You're too close to Ms. Vazquez," Kincaid continues. "You compromise everyone by going in."

They're absolutely right, but I don't have to like it.

"You," Kincaid says, turning his attention to Max, "need to lay low. The FBI doesn't know exactly who we're going after since we know there are at least half a dozen women in the compound, but I don't imagine there's any point in shoving you in their face. If things go wrong in there, we risk burning eleven UCs and years' worth of work."

Max opens his mouth to argue.

"I'm not saying you can't come with us to Florida. I respect your position both as Mia's brother and a former FBI agent, but you will not get in the way."

Max nods, not completely satisfied but unwilling to argue with the men agreeing to rescue his sister.

"And if she's not in the compound?"

It's the same question I wanted to ask myself but was going to wait until Max wasn't around in case the answer isn't one he wants to hear.

"Then we keep looking until we do," Dominic says.

Chapter 25

Jasmine

"Crap," I mutter as I walk into the clubhouse and see everyone hanging out in the living room.

Well, not everyone. Not one Cerberus guy is around, so either they've been run off, or they left town. The fear that Max once talked about feeling when Kingston was deployed hits me in the chest for the first time. It seems no matter how much I want to distance myself from everything involving those two men; my heart just won't let me.

"You don't seem very happy to see us," Camryn says as she pats the sofa cushion right beside her.

"I came to help take down the decorations," I lie as I cross the room.

"If that were true," Ivy begins, "you would've been here yesterday."

"Exactly," Camryn says, pointing at Ivy.

"Where's Jameson?" I ask Gigi.

She raises an eyebrow at me, and I realize I must be as transparent as glass.

"You mean, where's Tug?" Gigi counters.

"Umm…"

"If you gals are going to start talking about girly shit, then I'm leaving," Cannon complains.

He looks around the room for support, but Griffin and Samson don't seem as eager to leave their girls.

"You wouldn't believe how fun it is," my sister says as she and Izzy walk toward us from the kitchen.

"You'll have to shoot me a link," Izzy tells her with a smile.

The grin on my sister's face falls the second she sees me sitting on the sofa. Her arms cross over her chest, and I glare at Cannon when his eyes focus on the way her stubborn stance is making her breasts lift higher.

"Chill," Griffin says as he lifts his leg and strikes Cannon's shin with the tip of his boot.

"Fucker," Cannon hisses, but at least he pulls his eyes from my baby sister long enough to pull up the leg of his jeans to inspect for damage.

"We need to talk," Sophia says as she plops down beside Gigi.

"Should I go?" Izzy draws everyone's attention when she speaks and hitches her thumb over her shoulder.

"Stay," Sophia says without pulling her eyes from my face. "We're all adults here. Go on."

Sophia's eyes urge me to talk, but I wouldn't have this conversation with her alone much less in front of all of these people. Has she lost her damn mind?

"The wedding was gorgeous," I say instead.

"It was beyond magical," Camryn agrees. "Delilah knew exactly what she wanted, and I'm so glad everyone was able to make it happen for her."

"Where did they go for their honeymoon?" I ask.

"They're spending a week in Denver but have plans for a longer vacation in the summer after she graduates."

Gigi chuckles and Griffin does just about the same thing only the sound comes out in a rush of air from his nose. These people aren't idiots. They know what Camryn and I are trying to do. I would wager they were all talking about what happened last night within minutes of Kingston, Max, and I walking out of here.

"I've got all damn day," Sophia spits.

Even Cannon looks across the living room at me with a salacious smile on his face. He doesn't seem too eager to scurry away now that two single and gorgeous women have joined the group. He's as hungry for the gossip as everyone else, but what they don't understand is that while they speak amongst themselves about this kind of stuff, I was never a part of this group. There is too much of an age gap. Even if my extracurricular activities have brought my business a little closer to home, it doesn't give them the right to demand the details.

"I've got nothing to say," I tell my sister.

"Mom and Dad had plenty to say when they got home last night."

My eyes narrow. She's drawing me in. She's an expert in this tactic. She knows I want to know what people say about me, and this little crumb is enough to pique my interest.

"What did they say?"

Sophia looks around the group as if she's questioning me if I want her to say the things out loud in front of them. She thrives on fear, so I cock an eyebrow in challenge.

My demeanor is in contrast to the pounding in my heart. I'm not ashamed of what I've done with the guys. If it were just Camryn and me, I'd go into as much detail as she wanted, but even though we grew up together, this isn't my group of people. Hell, maybe they are. I don't really have a group of people. Most of my free time the last couple of years has been spent at sex clubs and in anonymous encounters with men I only see once or twice.

"They were both extremely shocked to bust in on you while you sucked two guys off," Sophia says. At first, I think she's angry, but the tone of her voice tells me she's more intrigued than anything else.

"Nice," Gigi says with a wide smile.

"Really?" Cannon's eyes dart down to my tight t-shirt before finding my eyes again. As hard as he tries, his gaze settles on my mouth.

"Umm..." It's clear that Ivy isn't as comfortable with this subject.

"I forgot I have laundry to do," Izzy says before she darts out of the room.

"Cannon, act like an adult, or leave the room," Griffin warns.

"Seriously?" I huff. "This isn't any of us acting like adults. Grown people don't sit around and talk about their sex lives with their friends."

I look to Camryn to make sure she has my back, but her lip curls up in disagreement.

"Really?"

Everyone nods, Cannon more enthusiastically than everyone else.

"Did you and Tug have something going on before you went to the club?" Sophia asks.

"No," I answer before I can stop myself.

"I can't wait to go," my little sister says, wistfully.

"What?" Ivy gasps. "You wouldn't."

Cannon rubs his hands together like an evil mastermind.

"Of course, I would," Sophia assures Ivy.

"It's a pretty fun place," Gigi adds. "I hear Gus is running things over there right now."

"Impossible," I argue. "There's no way Denver Police Lieutenant Kaleb Perez would allow his firstborn son to run a sex club."

"Allow?" Gigi says. "He's Griffin's age. A grown man already out of college. I'm sure it's a lucrative business. His dad should be proud."

I frown at her after realizing another damn judgmental stereotype just came out of my mouth. *How can I expect people to be okay with my lifestyle when I always seem to have a negative opinion about what everyone else is doing in theirs?*

"He's sexy as sin is what he is," Sophia says. If we were in the middle of a cartoon, she'd have little pink hearts floating about her head.

"And he's your fucking cousin," Gigi reminds her.

"So?" Sophia counters. "I can still appreciate his good looks."

"Shouldn't do it out loud," I mutter.

I didn't have a damn clue that Gus was running things over there. If I had, I probably would've avoided the place. Wouldn't want to chance hooking up with family. He's only related to me technically by marriage, but still, the thought of touching him sexually makes my skin crawl.

"Dylan is the sexiest one there," Gigi adds.

"The bartender?" I ask, fine with the direction this conversation is going.

I'm okay talking about the club in general; I just don't want to speak of my time and activities there.

"Yeah. Rosco is pretty hot, too."

"Rosco?"

"The guy at the front." Gigi leans in closer to me. "What color bands do you get?"

"You first," I challenge.

"Purple," she says with a shrug. "Jameson would throw a fit if I even hinted at wanting something else."

"Do you?"

Her head shakes, and it's then that I realize how in love those two are. Many people can have a baby together and it would only weaken their bond, but I have a feeling that although Amelia is a blessing, their forever was written in stone before the two lines showed up on the pregnancy test.

"Spill." Gigi kicks her leg back at me, refusing to let me get away without answering.

"Green and purple."

Her eyes close as her lips move. It's as if she's running the list through in her mind.

"Oh!" she squeals. "So that's how you ended up with two."

A wicked smile plays at her lips, and it makes me feel like a jerk all over again. This woman has found the love of her life, but she has no problem, no judgment being excited that I found something that doesn't look exactly like the cookie-cutter relationship that she has.

"So green is for a threesome? What is purple for?" Sophia asks.

I'd refuse to answer her, but Camryn leans a little closer to hear my answer as well.

"Purple is for exhibitionism," Gigi answers. "It means people like to be watched while messing around."

"I can't believe Jameson allows that," Griffin grumbles as he pulls Ivy closer to his chest.

That action alone proves that the man would never be okay with anyone seeing his girl in such a passionate, vulnerable way. To each their own.

"And green?" Sophia repeats.

"Green isn't for threesomes," I begin, "it's for group sex."

It's comical the way my sister's jaw nearly unhinges. "Group? As in more than three?"

"My dick's hard," Cannon whispers.

"For fuck's sake," Samson says, throwing an empty water bottle at Cannon's head.

"Language," Griffin snaps at his best friend.

Not all Marines are created equal, I guess. Kingston wouldn't bat an eyelash at the filthy talk. Hell, he's a fan of it himself, and I have to say the way he's spoken to both Max and me on occasion makes me want to clench my thighs together. My heart is wanting to put up walls to keep them both out, but my body knows exactly what it wants from both of them.

Chapter 26

Max

"I feel helpless," I confess in a whisper to Kingston.

"Me too," he says.

We have hardly spoken to each other since we had the fight yesterday morning back at Jasmine's apartment. I don't blame him for being angry with me. I acted like a child, even though it was much the same way I acted when we were kids, and he's doing exactly the same thing. He'll keep his distance, punishing me for having an opinion about the situation until he thinks I've had enough.

I'd planned to apologize last night, but Cerberus put me up in a room alone while Kingston was with one of the guys on the infiltration team. Kincaid, Dominic, and Shadow have accompanied us, something I take as unusual these days. Kingston seemed shocked when they climbed into an SUV to caravan among the others to the private airstrip on the other side of town.

I don't know whether to be glad to have the additional support or be concerned that the situation is so bad they feel the need to tag along. It's just one more thing I haven't had the chance to ask Kingston.

"Forty-five seconds," Shadow says. "Godspeed, guys."

I see the leader of the line using hand signals to instruct the men behind him. They're each wearing a ton of gear and cameras on their helmets. Even though we're standing in the command center a few blocks away, it's almost as if we're there with them.

The shuffle of their feet is nearly silent as Cerberus makes it past the four guards at the front gate without so much as a grunt from any of them. They keep to the shadows before spreading out to cover the different points of entry.

My foot taps an anxious rhythm until Kingston presses his warm palm on my knee.

"Maybe you should step outside," he suggests, but I can't take my eyes off the screen.

I thought watching and not arguing to be there would give me the distance I needed to prepare me for the worst in case things don't go the way we want them to, but the technology is just too good.

"I'm fine," I assure him, but I can tell by the way his fingers clench my kneecap that he knows I'm full of shit.

"Kitchen and dining room clear," one of the guys says into his mic.

The next couple of minutes are spent suspended in anticipation as they make their way through the compound.

Periodically, the sounds of a scuffle are heard, but the targets are taken out systematically.

"What the fuck?" comes from one mic as one of the Cerberus guys pushes open a door.

His camera focuses on the biggest man I've ever seen as he shoves his hips forward and back.

A muffled shot rings out, and the beast of a man falls to the floor. The camera then angles down as the Cerberus guy checks for a pulse. His hand stops before reaching her skin. It's clear the woman has been dead for a while.

"He was fucking a gash in her side," the Cerberus guy says.

"That was Miguel 'Toro' Montoya," Shadow says into his mic at the back of our room.

"The Bull," I mutter. "Who was the girl?"

"Keep moving, Jinx," Shadow urges the guy we've been focused on.

The camera shakes up and down as if the guy is nodding his assent.

I can't take it anymore. The woman on that table could easily be Mia. I'm walking toward the door to exit the command center when there is a rash of yells and curses.

More shots ring out as I turn to look at the eight screens displaying what each Cerberus member is seeing and going through.

"Rocker's hit." That's Scooter's voice, and he's calmer than I could ever be in this very situation.

"Report," Shadow demands.

"H-hit my vest."

"Lay low, Rocker. Let them finish this, and then we can get you out of there," Shadow instructs.

Another barrage of bullets fly and it makes my skin crawl. Our guys' weapons don't sound like that. They're taking on heavy enemy fire, but as soon as it starts, it's over.

A door shoves open on one of the screens, and more than a dozen women crouched in fear come into view. They whimper, but none of them scream at the men walking into the room in full combat gear. The things these women must've been through.

One by one the other cameras focus on the women, but they're all filthy, damn near starved to death and huddled so close to each other that you can't tell one person from the next.

For the next half hour, we don't hear shit. Kingston tries to explain that this is part of it.

"Even pulling the women out of there doesn't mean that they will talk to us. Sometimes it takes weeks before we're able to get proper identification on them. They've been to hell and back, and trust is something they no longer have. Even when the guys in the white hats show up."

The cameras are still running, but I had to turn my back on the visual a while ago. As someone with a more technical background in the FBI, I normally only heard of places like this. I've never watched this kind of thing in my life. I can't even begin to imagine what these women will go through, even after being rescued.

"Mia?"

"Scooter, do you have her?" Shadow asks. He hasn't taken his eyes off the screens even though the guys were safe and beginning to escort the women from the premises.

"Mia Vazquez?"

Hearing my sister's full name has me turning to face the screen once again. The woman on Scooter's camera no longer looks like my sister. The long, dark, gorgeous hair she always had in a messy knot on the top of her head is cut short, sheered to the scalp in places. She's covered in more filth and grime than we managed when Ma and Pa let us play in the mud when it rained as kids. Her arm, although bandaged is clearly broken. All of that is awful, but it's the deadness in her eyes when Scooter bends down to get eye level with her that breaks my fucking heart.

"That's her," I sob. "That's Mia."

"I'm going to pick you up, Mia," Scooter says as he reaches out his arms to her.

She doesn't flinch or try to shy away. She's a stone, a block of ice with no emotions as he lifts her and turns to carry her out of the room.

"I have to go to her."

A strong hand clamps on my arm. "She's going to need medical attention first."

I turn to face Kingston. His face is ashen-white, having seen what I just saw.

"She's dead inside," I tell him.

"A lot of them are by the time we get to them," he confesses. "Let the medical personnel take care of her. We have to address her physical injuries before we can even begin to work on the emotional and mental aspects of what this has done to her."

It's the last thing I want to do. In my mind, just rushing to her to let her know that I'm going to be there for her every step of the way will be enough to bring her back to the land of the living. But deep down, I know better.

"Let's head to the hospital," Kingston suggests. "That way we can be close when she's ready for visitors."

I nod, letting him guide me out of the command center to an SUV.

Even at four in the morning, Miami traffic is a headache. The hospital the women are being taken to is on the opposite side of town from where the compound is. Cerberus didn't want to take any chances that Jiménez had connections that would cause problems at the closest medical center.

"She has to be okay," I say more to myself than to Kingston.

He doesn't respond, doesn't placate me with words of support or fake assurances that everything will be fine. Neither one of us knows that for sure.

"We'll do everything in our power to make sure she's okay," he says instead.

Tears stream down my face as we park outside of the hospital. I don't make a move to get out of the vehicle, well aware that we will have hours of waiting ahead of us before we're given a chance to go to her.

"Come here," Kingston says as he shoves up the console between us.

I don't hesitate for a second before sliding into his arms. The warmth of his body only makes the sobs grow in strength. Guilt barrels over me, knowing that I led those sick bastards to my sister's doorstep. If I hadn't been greedy in keeping such a close eye on her, she would still be at home planning her wedding.

"I wish she were here," I whisper into his neck.

"Me too," he responds, somehow knowing that I'm talking about Jasmine. "We both owe her an apology."

I nod in agreement against his skin.

"I don't know yet what we're apologizing for, but it'll go a long way in making her understand that we want her."

"Need her," I correct.

"Yeah," he agrees as his arms hold me tighter.

Chapter 27

Tug

"Is this normal?" Max asks as he looks around the men filling the waiting room.

"Yes. Unless it's impossible, we always wait until the last rescue has been treated."

"Oh." Max hangs his head once again.

He looks so lost with his elbows on his knees and head angled down. We're all exhausted, having been in the waiting room since shortly after Mia was brought in and assessed. She was immediately taken back to surgery for the injury to her arm.

"I need to tell you something," I begin after hours and hours of silence.

He doesn't lift his head or acknowledge me.

"Come with me." I shove at his shoulder to get his attention.

I know he isn't sleeping. He lifts his head every time the doors going back to the operating room swing open.

"Where are we going?" he asks when I grip his shirt and haul him to his feet when he doesn't make a move to follow me.

Other than going outside, there isn't really a place to talk as privately as I'd like, and I know Max doesn't want to get too far from the doors the doctor is expected to come through to give us information on Mia.

"What?" he hisses when I push him against the side of a vending machine.

Gone is the crying man that clung to my shirt in the SUV several hours ago. He's been replaced with the angry version of Max. Normally, I'd be okay with facing the angry side of a person going through tragedy, but Max's angry side is irrational. Max's angry side has the potential to start a war. This isn't a good thing for anyone involved.

"Calm down," I urge.

His venomous eyes snap to mine, but I don't cower. How can I when I'm full of the same hatred for what's happened to Mia? It's always hard to face what people are capable of in the world, but to be hit in the face by it from being someone you know and love, that's almost impossible to deal with.

"I called your parents."

"You did what?" he roars.

I hold my hand up when Shadow steps around the vending machine to make sure everything is alright.

"They have a right to know that Mia has been found. They were hopping on the first plane they could get," I continue.

Might as well lay it all out right now. This way, he can get angry with me once.

"How long ago was that?" He glares at me, but I don't back down.

"Four hours ago," I admit. "I got a text fifteen minutes ago that they had landed."

"Are you purposely trying to make me hate you?"

His question takes me by surprise, so I do the only thing I can think to settle him down. I lift my hand and cup his cheek. Surprisingly, he doesn't swat my arm away. He leans into my touch as I pull him closer with my other arm.

"You're going to have to face them eventually," I whisper in his ear.

The scruff on his jaw tangles with the scruff on mine. It's like even our facial hair is holding on to each other. It's such an odd thing to realize as his breathing begins to even out. I know we're heading in the right direction when his arms circle my waist as well.

"We'll get through this together," I assure him.

"I'm not worried about us," he confesses. "I'm terrified Mia will never be the same."

I take a step back, so he can look in my eyes. "Mia will never be the same. You have to accept that now. Hopefully, she'll be okay eventually, but expecting her to bounce back one hundred percent from this is unrealistic."

"I would do anything to have taken her place."

I wipe away the tear from his cheek before it makes it all the way down to his chin.

"I know. I would, too."

My hand is once again on his jaw, and my best friend is looking up at me like I have the ability to fix it all. Since I know I can't, I cup his jaw and lower my lips to his. It's the only peace I can offer him.

The kiss is soft, almost chaste, but important none the less.

A throat clearing makes me pull my head away, but I don't snap to attention or shove Max away. The urge to distance myself to keep others from suspecting what may be going on disappeared hours ago.

Shadow looks at both of us before focusing on me. "Mr. and Mrs. Vazquez are here."

It isn't until tension tightens Max's muscles that I realize I still have him in my arms.

"Thank you," I tell Shadow before looking back at Max. "Are you ready?"

His head begins to shake violently. "I can't see them. They've been through enough."

"Max," I chide. "You have to face them."

"I can't."

"I won't lie to them."

"I just need a little more time." Without another word, he walks away.

"Is that your new boyfriend?"

I spin around to face Ramon and Estella Vazquez. My head snaps in Max's direction, and we all watch his dark head disappear around a corner.

"It's so good to see you." I shake Ramon's hand before kissing Estella's cheek and giving her a hug, all the while avoiding the question.

Just like when I was younger, she wraps her arms around me and holds me tighter than it looks like she's capable of doing.

"How is she?" Ramon asks.

"Let's head into the consultation room so we can talk." I lead the way down the opposite hall that Max disappeared to and push open the door to the small conference area the doctor assured us we could use to contact family members of the victims.

"Would you like some water?" I offer, pointing to the small cooler against the far side of the wall.

"No, thank you," they both respond before taking seats at the small oval table in the center of the room.

"Please tell us what's going on?"

"Hello?" An unfamiliar man pokes his head in the door.

"We're busy," I snap. Don't people fucking knock anymore? I could be delivering crushing news right now.

"Hold on." Estella raises her hand and urges the man forward. "This is Mia's fiancé, Jason Sealey. He was parking the rental car."

"Kingston Jacks," I tell him, offering my hand and a look of apology.

"Please tell us," Ramon urges again.

"She's in surgery for a compound fracture of her left arm. She's dehydrated, malnourished, and has been to hell and back."

"But she's going to live?" Jason asks. It's clear by the concern in his eyes that he loves her. "Is she?"

It's the question we get most often from family members. They don't have a clue what their loved ones have been through, and that's an honest blessing, but it also doesn't help them prepare for the aftermath either.

"Physically, Mia is expected to make a full recovery. But—"

The door snaps open, and I'm seeing red when I turn around to beat the shit out of the person interrupting us now.

Max doesn't look at me when he steps into the room. His focus is one hundred percent on his parents.

"Ma? Pa?"

Both of them stare in shock, while Jason looks like he's seen a ghost. It seems like time slows to a crawl as they watch each other. I'm worried for Estella as she clutches her chest, but realize she's going after her rosary rather than trying to tell us she's having a heart attack.

"Maximiliano?" his dad whispers as if thinking if he speaks too loud, his son will turn into mist and disappear.

"It's me, Pa."

"But you died," his mother gasps.

"It's a long story," Max says.

"Max?" Jason stands from the chair beside Estella. "As in Mia's twin that died ten years ago?"

Max looks between the stranger and his parents, but they're still in shock over his resurrection.

"Nice to meet—"

Before Max can extend his hand all the way to shake his sister's fiancé's hand, Jason pulls his fist back and slams it into Max's jaw. Then as if he was never there, the guy walks out of the room.

As if the slamming of the conference room door was a bell, both Ramon and Estella snap out of their trances and wrap their son in a hug. I back out of the room and give them the time they need. Max has a lot of explaining to do, and it's not my story to tell.

Chapter 28

Max

My mother hasn't stopped crying since she saw me for the first time earlier. Just when I thought she was coming to the end of it, her muffled whimpers were renewed when we were finally able to wait by Mia's bed for her to wake up. We've been in here for an hour and a half, and my sister still hasn't so much as twitched.

What I thought was filth and dirt on my sister's face from the video feed is actually layer after layer of bruising. She's a tiny thing in the hospital bed with dozens of cords and wires coming off of her frail body. The arm that was operated on is in a huge bandage, and it's the only thing I can really focus on since the doctor gave us an update and walked out to see to the plethora of other patients they were inundated with after the compound was raided.

Her fiancé, later introduced to me as Jason Sealey, stands with his arms crossed against the far wall. He may have gotten the one-shot in on me, but he's kept his distance ever since. I can feel his eyes burning in the back of my head, but I don't give him the time of day.

"Here."

I turn to the tap on my shoulder to find Kingston standing beside me with a steaming cup of coffee in his hand.

"Thanks," I mutter as I take the peace offering.

I don't know why I'm still mad at him for calling my parents. Deep down, I know they have a right to know about Mia. I knew I was going to have to face them and my decade worth of lies, eventually. I just feel like he blindsided me. There is so much shit to stress over; I don't know where my focus should be.

Quiet whispers fill the room as Kingston and my parents begin talking again. Jason doesn't join in this time, and I know it's killing him not being closer to my sister. Ma assured me that the punch he threw was completely out of character for him, but the force he hit my jaw with tells a different story. I'm concocting all sorts of things in my head about the man. It's the only thing keeping me sane, especially with the continuous beep, beep, beep of the fucking machine tracking Mia's heart rate.

"Wanna take a walk? Get some circulation in your legs?" Kingston is close to my ear, and as much as I love the warmth of his breath on my face, I'm incapable of pulling my eyes from my sister, terrified that if I look away, she'll be the one to disappear.

"I'm gonna stay."

"I think Jason would like a few moments alone with her," he says softly.

"I'm her brother," I argue.

"He's the man she's chosen to spend the rest of her life with," he replies.

"I'm not leaving."

In the next instant, he's gone. Kingston knows better than to push when I've dug my feet in.

Mia's palm twitches in mine, so I lean in closer and speak to her in a hushed voice.

I lost track of what I was telling her about before, so I speak of all the things we can do when she gets out of here. I share promises of long walks, movie marathons, and a shopping spree, all the things she wanted to do when we were younger.

Her lips twitch as if she's trying to smile, but then it's followed by a painful groan from her dry throat.

"Don't try to move," I beg when her eyes flutter open and close several times before she holds them open completely. Her head rolls on the bed as she makes eye contact with me.

"Max." Her voice is a cracked garble, but her lips move again to smile. "I knew I would see you again."

I squeeze her hand harder, my own tears threatening to fall when wetness creeps past her blinking eyelids. The tears make trails over the discolored patches of skin on her face. Some old, some new, but every injury to her is cataloged in my mind.

"I didn't think Heaven would be so painful," she mutters, wincing as she tries to move. "For weeks, I begged them to kill me. I'm so glad they finally did."

My mother gasps a sob just as Jason steps from the corner, inching closer to the bed.

"Ma? Pa?" my sister says as she looks in their direction with exhausted eyes. "Jason?"

Confused, my sister's eyes dart back to mine, and I can see what's going to happen before she rips her hands from mine. Knowing she's about to break doesn't do anything to ease the pain of watching it happen. Coming here was a mistake. Seeing me again is just too much for her mind to handle. I knew it, but I let Kingston tell me otherwise. I love my family but staying dead to them was always better.

The first scream that rips from her lips is hoarse and less than half of what she's capable of. The second one is stronger, and by the fourth, I'm surprised the roof isn't caving in on us.

"Mia?" Jason steps closer, reaching for her hand, trying to soothe her.

It doesn't work.

My mother and father's approach do nothing either. She's inconsolable. She's curling in on herself, making it impossible for anyone to touch her. She's tucked into a tiny ball on the bed, and I stand here helpless, unable to think of anything to make her understand no one is going to hurt her here.

"What the fuck?" Scooter asks as he pushes through all of us.

I'm thinking he's just one more person watching my sister fall apart, but at the sound of his voice, Mia snaps her head in his direction. Instead of cringing away, she reaches her arms out to him. It's reminiscent of a terrified baby reaching toward the safety of her mother's arms.

"Shh, Mia. I got you." Scooter doesn't waste a second climbing on the bed with her and letting my sister fold herself around his body. He's aware of the wires coming off her but manages to settle her against his chest without disturbing any of them.

"Do they know each other?" Jason asks with more ire than belongs in this room.

"Yes," Kingston says before I can answer. "He's her savior."

No one else says a word. We all stare in shock as Scooter smooths his rough hand over Mia's patchy head in a calming pattern. Eventually, her sobs grow quiet, and the tears stop flowing down her bruised cheeks. His hand never falters. Over the back of her head and down her back, only to be lifted and repeated. Over and over and over. He doesn't tire as she relaxes in his arms and her breathing softens.

"Can someone please tell me what's going on?" Jason whisper hisses.

Scooter doesn't even bother to lift his head. His lips move with words so soft, no one but a sleeping Mia can hear.

"Has she been having an affair with that man?"

"That's it," I hiss, but Kingston has a hold of Jason's collar and is dragging him from the room before I get a chance to do it myself.

"Now isn't the time for misplaced jealousy," Kingston says as he releases Jason with a shove.

The man's shoes squeak on the linoleum before he gains his balance. He doesn't raise his fist to Kingston the way he did to me earlier. At least the man isn't a complete idiot.

"She seems really cozy with him," Jason spits from a couple of feet away.

"Scooter is the one who rescued her," Kingston explains. "This happens sometimes. An attachment is formed temporarily with the person who brings someone back from hell."

"I'm her fiancé."

"And she isn't the same woman she was seven weeks ago before she was abducted," I tell him.

Now I understand Kingston's reluctance in telling me everything would be okay.

Jason swallows roughly, and I can tell it's killing him not to be in there with Mia. Only I can't tell if it's because he loves her like he should or if he's bitterly jealous that he wasn't the one she reached for during the middle of her crisis.

"You need to give her some space," Kingston says.

"It should be me," he argues. "I should be the one comforting her."

"You don't need to interfere. Scooter will take care of her."

"Like hell."

Kingston steps into Jason's path, preventing him from going back into the room.

"Is there a problem here?" Two security guards face us, most likely having been called for Mia's outburst.

"The patient doesn't want to see this man. Please keep him off the floor until Ms. Vazquez requests otherwise."

"You can't do this!" Jason roars at Kingston, but he doesn't fight the men who urge him toward the elevator.

I feel like I'm seconds away from crashing, but that doesn't stop me from stepping toward Mia's door once again to watch her. Scooter's mouth is still moving; his hand still tracing the back of her head and her spine. My father is softly consoling my mom who sobs quietly near the window.

"We're debriefing," Kingston says as he steps up beside me before putting his cell phone back in his pocket. "Want to tag along?"

I nod and let him guide me away from my sister. She's never going to forgive me for my role in this, and I can't say that I blame her.

Chapter 29

Tug

Uncaring of who sees us, I wrap my arm around Max as we walk back toward the conference room. When Kincaid and Dominic got back from finishing up at the compound, they commandeered this room.

"Scooter can't make it," I tell them as we walk inside.

"We heard." Shadow dips his head at Max in solidarity.

Midday sun is streaming through the single window of the room, but no matter what time of day, everyone in this room is nearly dead on their feet. Striking the compound in the early hours of the morning was optimal, but we've been setting things in motion since I woke up yesterday under Max's body.

"Stats?" Rocker asks on a wheeze.

He took a couple of shots to the chest, but other than a couple serious bruises, he's fine. He'll hurt like hell for a couple days, but by the time the next jobs rolls in, he'll be itching to go again.

"Twenty-four cartel members dead, including Miguel 'Toro' Montoya. Good job on that one, Jinx," Shadow praises.

Several guys clap him on the back, but Jinx, after walking in on what he did, is in no mood to celebrate.

"We discovered three deceased females," Shadow continues. "Luis Jiménez wasn't in the compound."

Shadow waits until the cussing and grumbles subside.

"Seventeen women were rescued."

Another round of cheers. It's not the most we've pulled from a job like this, but it may be the biggest one on domestic soil.

"A cache of weapons, more kilos of cocaine than the DEA can count, and several million dollars in cash were also confiscated."

Max doesn't even smile when the guys celebrate.

"Also," the room settles in an instant the moment Kincaid opens his mouth, "the woman in the room with The Bull was Special Agent Sara DeMoss. According to initial reports she'd been dead for several days."

"That means—" Jinx begins.

"That sick fuck," Rocker hisses.

"That's not all," Kincaid says. "Special Agent Gabriella Butler is still in the wind. Early intel says that Jiménez may be heading to Venezuela. Security footage from the FBI makes it clear that Agent Butler was with him ten hours ago."

"So, we're heading back to South America?" Jinx asks.

Kincaid nods.

"Glad I won't fucking miss it this time," Grinch says.

"We'll head that way after Christmas," Shadow says.

"After?" I ask as several of the other guys grumble their displeasure as well.

"Agent Butler…" Shadow sighs.

"She was placed on this assignment because she looks like Luis' mother," Max adds when it doesn't seem like Shadow wants to explain. Either that, or he doesn't have all the information.

"She's old?" one of the guys asks.

"Luis' was in a sexual relationship with his mother since he was a teen. His father murdered her in front of him when they were caught a couple of years ago," Max continues. "Butler was sent in with the hope that he would attach himself to her and make it easier for her to gain intel."

"The FBI thinks she's been turned," Kincaid says. "Someone tipped Jiménez off, and with Agent DeMoss down, that only left Butler in the compound—"

"I manufactured Butler's identity," Max interrupts with a shaky voice. "Is that why they went after my sister?"

"No," Shadow answers succinctly. "Your sister's abduction had nothing to do with your link to the FBI. As far as we can tell, she was in the wrong place at the wrong time."

"What?" Max asks.

Kincaid steps a few feet closer to Max. "According to FBI records and a conversation I had with DEA Agent Munoz, Mia was taken to be trafficked, not to be tortured for information on you."

"Oh, God." Max covers his mouth like he's going to be sick, and I know what's killing him.

Trafficked women go through hell, but what he doesn't fully understand is that these women are merchandise. Had she been taken for the reason he suspected; she would already be dead. It was what I tried to explain to him in the beginning, and he wouldn't listen to me.

Jinx clears his throat. "Are you sure we have to wait until after the holidays?"

"Yeah," Shadow answers, but even he doesn't sound happy about it. "We have to verify Butler's involvement, and their move to Cortez's compound complicates things."

"Which Cortez?" Rockers snaps.

"Luis," Kincaid answers.

"Motherfucker," several guys mutter.

When they went on their last mission to South America, they were able to recover a couple of abducted women. The little girl they were after was already dead. Her little body incapable of handling the torture, the dozens of men who paid, inflicted on her. Only one of the girls from the mission group was rescued. The other girl hasn't been located yet.

To say that they were pissed about what went down would be an understatement.

"How are they connected?" I ask, expecting to get an answer from Shadow or Kincaid.

"They're first cousins," Max answers instead. "Their mothers were sisters."

"I want to kill them all," Jinx says.

Several guys agree with him before Kincaid raises his hand to silence everyone.

"We have a lot of shit to get together. They will have reinforced both Cortez compounds. We will get no local help. The death of that little girl will be enough to frighten the people of those villages for generations to come. I want to stop each and every bad guy in this world, but I won't do it at the risk of losing a single one of you guys. We're heading home. Some of you guys are spreading out to see family. I want everyone to reconvene back at the clubhouse on January second. Hopefully by then, we'll have our dossiers, and we'll be in a better place to take these fuckers down."

"Those heading back to New Mexico, the plane leaves in an hour and a half. That gives you enough time to hit the hotel, gather your shit and get on board," Shadow adds as everyone begins to stand.

"Have them wait for me," I tell Rocker before he can leave.

He nods and walks past. I grab Max's hand and drag him back down by the vending machine we were standing by earlier.

"I need to get back to Mia." He pinches the bridge of his nose in frustration.

"It wasn't your fault," I remind him.

I know it won't help right now, while Mia is still in a hospital bed, but eventually, the information will sink in, and it'll be easier for him to live with himself.

"Are you coming back with me?" Hope fills my voice, but I already know the answer before the full question leaves my mouth.

"I need to be here for my family." He refuses to look me in the eye, and I already feel him pulling away from me.

My heart beats harder in my chest.

"I have to figure out what the rest of my future looks like. I'm no longer an agent. No longer Rodrigo Flores, and Maximiliano Vazquez is dead." He draws in a ragged breath. "I don't know what the hell is going to happen now."

"You're always welcome with me in New Mexico," I offer.

He huffs a humorless laugh. "Want me to wait in the bed for you with my mouth open, ready to take your cock while you run around the world saving women and doing something that matters?"

"That's not what I meant," I argue.

"That's what will happen if I end up there. I'm no one's kept man."

I can't think of a single thing to offer him instead. He'd never be happy with any type of job that Farmington could offer him. The idea of him teaching computer classes at the college Jasmine works at is completely ridiculous. Max would strangle a whiny teen as soon as look at one.

"I don't want to lose you again," I confess.

"Thank you." His hand cups my cheek. "Thank you for helping find Mia. Thank you for being the man I always knew you were."

"Wh-why does this feel like goodbye?"

He doesn't respond. Max merely presses his lips to my scruffy jaw before walking away.

"Let's roll," Kincaid says as he walks by.

Knowing now isn't the time for a confrontation, I follow my boss out to the waiting SUVs rather than my love down the hospital corridor.

Scooter comes out a few steps behind us, and the sound of his cell phone ringing draws both mine and Kincaid's eyes. When Scooter looks up from his phone to our boss, Kincaid simply nods his head. Scooter turns on his heel and runs back into the hospital. Two minutes later we're riding out of the parking lot without him.

"Why didn't you stay here, dude?" Rocker asks from beside me.

"I need to get back home," I tell him, but the truth of it is, Max didn't offer. I knew if I invited myself, he'd say some terrible things, and I'm not at a place that I can handle that right now. He knows where I'm at, and when he's done acting like he's shouldering the entire weight of the world, I'll be in New Mexico waiting for him. With any luck and a little hope, I'm praying I can convince Jasmine to be waiting for him, too.

Even the safety of the private jet wouldn't allow any form of rest as we left the warmth of Miami in winter and flew straight back to the private airstrip on the outskirts of Farmington. We were dead on our feet, but that didn't stop each and every one of us from running scenarios through our heads as to how we will handle shit in South America in less than two weeks. We all know that waiting and gathering information is vital for a successful mission, but we also know that sometimes striking when the iron is hot could mean success, as well.

"Ride with us," Kincaid says as we drag our asses off the plane.

"Yes, sir," I answer even though the sight of Dominic climbing into the driver's seat makes me question if I'll ever see the inside of my room at Cerberus again.

"Where are you headed for the holiday?" Kincaid asks when we close ourselves in Dominic's SUV.

"I don't have plans, sir."

Jasmine's dad's eyes find mine in the rearview mirror.

"The family is getting together at the clubhouse."

It's not an invite exactly, so I don't have any idea what he expects me to say.

"We expect Jasmine to be there on time," Kincaid says, but his eyes stay focused out the front windshield.

"Lunch at twelve hundred hours. Presents start at fourteen hundred," Dominic grunts.

"Makayla likes boots. Size eight," Kincaid adds.

"But gift cards are nice, too." Dominic looks almost pained handing over this information.

"What does Jasmine like?"

I hate myself for asking the question the second it leaves my mouth.

I should fucking know what she likes.

"You should fucking know what she likes," Dominic snaps.

His foot comes off the gas, and I wonder if this is the point where he plans to kill me and dump my body.

Unwilling to back down, I keep my eyes on his in the rearview mirror until we come to a complete stop.

"Get out," he grunts.

"What?"

"Out, and the next time I see my little girl, she better not have tears in her eyes."

When my feet hit the ground, I realize that they've dropped me off at the gate of Jasmine's apartment complex instead of the clubhouse. If this and the invite to celebrate Christmas with them, albeit in the most fucked up fashion ever, isn't Dominic giving me his blessing, then I don't know how he could've said it any simpler.

I make easy work of the gate, taking my time to walk through the darkness until I'm near Jasmine's apartment. There are no lights on in her place, and I'm only mildly scared that she'll shoot me when I open the door.

My heart is racing, my mouth unsure of what I can say to get her back, so I take the stairs one at a time as I work through my *please forgive me whatever it is that I've done* speech.

Chapter 30

Jasmine

I don't know if it's his scent hitting my nose or the rustle of my covers, but after two days of no contact, Kingston Jacks is climbing into my bed. My ears perk up, waiting to hear the sounds Max would make as he climbs in on the other side, but they never come.

I allow him to pull me to his chest, not only because I can't resist the warmth of his skin but also because I've been devastatingly lonely the last two days. Sure, I've spent time at the clubhouse and with my sister, but those encounters weren't what I've been craving.

I hate him. I hate both of them. I hate the way they managed to crawl under my skin to the point that I miss them even after being the one to shove them away. I don't have any right to act bitter or upset. I always knew it was going to be the two of them together. Their tale of destiny started when they were only kids. I have no claim to either one of them.

If only my heart would get the memo.

It's not love that I feel for them.

Hell, I don't even know how either one of them likes their eggs, but I yearn for them soul deep. Maybe it's more akin to an addiction, but no matter how someone from the outside looking in sees us, it doesn't really change my desire to have them both here with me.

Kingston's chest takes in ragged breaths, each one growing more fragmented as the seconds tick away.

"King?" I try to lift my head from his chest, but his grip around my body doesn't allow for it.

When a broken sob escapes his lips, it invites the pain and loss I've felt the last couple of days to come bubbling to the surface. I don't know why he's crying, but the fear that Mia is gone slams into my chest. Then I wonder selfishly if something happened to Max, as that seems to be the only conclusion I can come to that he wouldn't be here with Kingston and me.

"Is it Mia?" I ask, lifting my head from his chest after his anguish distracts his grip on me.

Tears streak down both sides of his face, and as heartbreaking as the sight of his pain is, the softness around his red-rimmed eyes is one of the most beautiful things I've ever seen. He's in pain, yet, he's here with me. He chose this bed, chose my arms to fall apart in. I can't help but read that as a sign.

"Talk to me," I urge as I lift my fingers to wipe away his tears.

Turning his head, Kingston brushes his lips on my palm. It's not the first time he's had his mouth on my skin, but the action is intimate, not sexual. Up until this point, his touches have been fevered, a promise of the pleasure to come. Right now? His unguarded eyes speak of something entirely different.

"What happened?" I press further.

His head shakes back and forth, but instead of letting the sting of rejection settle in my heart, I keep my eyes on his mouth, wondering if I'm brave enough to press my mouth to his for the first time, or if the chance of rejection is enough to keep me away.

I don't have to decide, however, because Kingston lifts his head and presses his mouth to mine. The first brush of his lips is filled with pain, and I inhale every ounce of it when I gasp at the contact. His breath rushes out, gusting from his nose, and for a split second, I wonder if he's trying to force this emotion to appease me.

But then he angles his head, letting his tongue sweep my lower lip, and as much as I claimed his attention right now wasn't sexual, the brief swipe of his tongue on my lip lights me on fire. My core clenches with needy anticipation, but I manage to hold still while he explores. Reading too much into what's happening would be my downfall.

"Jasmine," he moans against my lips in frustration when I hold steady and don't kiss him back. "Please."

The sorrowful tone of his voice brings my own serving of pain, and in the briefest of moments war wages in my head. Do I give in and see where this goes? Effectively, taking what he has to offer and expecting no more? Do I push him away and demand that he make some sort of declaration, force him to explain his intentions so I can make an informed decision?

Then the reasoning part of my brain explains that I have no right to demand anything from him. Our interactions were supposed to stay at the club. This right here is why I've always strived for anonymous sex. It's less messy. The expectations are clearly defined.

While the conflict is going on in my head, my body has taken over. My tongue is now moving with Kingston's, and my lower half is undulating and practically begging him to get ready for what I want.

"There you are," he whispers against my neck as his expert mouth licks and nips at the sensitive skin.

The grip of his bruising fingers on my skin set me on fire, and the only countermove I can manage is swiveling my hips and trying to gain purchase on his thigh.

He chuckles at my neediness, pressing a firm hand at my back to stop me from moving. "Slow down."

I pull my head away, ready to argue with him, but when his hooded eyes find mine, I'm once again lost.

I merely nod my agreement, and this must be exactly what he's been waiting for because he rolls me to my back and settles his large body between my slender thighs. For a split second, I think to be offended that he climbed into my bed naked, but who am I kidding? The fact that there's less to strip him out of is perfect. Instead, I'm mentally berating myself for putting panties on with my over-sized t-shirt this evening.

"Kiss me again," he urges with his lips only a breath away from mine.

My neck angles, closing the half-inch of distance between the two of us and the kiss is amazing, but it's the groan from his throat at the contact that makes my legs tighten around his waist.

He's not indifferent to my mouth on his. He's not suffering through the connection like I first worried about. He's thick and heavy between my legs, and although he's pressed against me, he isn't rooting and seeking.

He isn't spewing filthy words from his mouth or telling me what I'm going to do for him and how I'm going to love every second that he spends defiling me. He seems content to explore my mouth with his own, indulgent of the way he tangles his tongue with mine and the sips he's taking of my lips.

"Kingston," I whimper against his lips.

"Soon," he promises, before backing away a couple of inches and pulling my t-shirt off over my head.

When his lips find my nipple, his fingers dip lower and push down my panties. Just when I'm preparing for his swift invasion, he leans back on his knees, just staring at the sight of his cock resting against the silky lips of my sex. He doesn't move, doesn't shift his hips and run the crown of his cock up my slit. He merely watches.

And somehow, someway the inaction is sexier than if he was slamming inside of me. If getting wetter than drenched is possible, that's exactly what happens. My pussy quivers in need, but at the same time, staying stock still while he watches our flesh pressed against each other seems to be what he needs, so I give him this.

"You're gorgeous."

Pulling my eyes from the apex of my thighs, I expect to see him looking at the same thing, but he's looking directly into my eyes. Emotion clogs my throat as he leans closer and once again takes my mouth with his. A second later, a slow shift of his hips back and then forward begins his slow and torturous glide inside of me.

I've been fucked, pounded into without mercy, and I loved every second of it, but somehow the slow slide of him inside of me is the most erotic thing I've felt to date.

"Oh, God," I hiss when he seats himself fully.

It's everything. It's too much. It's not enough.

My body doesn't have a clue what's going on or what it needs, just more, more, more, and less, less, less.

When he pulls his hips back, it's torture, but then he presses forward again just as slowly. He maintains the dragging tempo with his mouth on mine, his fingers gripping my body, the brush of his groomed chest hair stimulating my nipples, and when he groans his pleasure, I feel it in every molecule of my own body.

"Come for me, baby," he insists, but as I'm getting ready to shake my head no, to open my mouth and tell him it isn't possible for me to climax with this languid speed, my body betrays me, obeying his command.

The detonation begins in my core before spilling out to my limbs, making the tips of my fingers and toes tingle with an energy that has nowhere else to go.

"That's it," he praises as I fall apart in his arms.

The orgasm is silent, only the rush of air escaping my mouth betraying the quake of my body into bliss.

His release isn't as serene. His jaw tightens, and no matter how slow and erotic he just made love to me, he can't keep his hips from slamming into me twice before his cock jerks deep in my core with his own climax.

His arms are trembling as out of character whimpers leave his lips. I don't call him on what just happened. I don't question the difference in him tonight compared to the other times we've spent time together. I don't tell him that it was amazing. Most importantly, I don't confess that even though it was incredible, that there's still something missing.

And when he crashes beside me on the bed and pulls me tight against his chest, neither one of us speaks of Max, even though we're both missing him right now.

Chapter 31

Tug

I don't know how long I've been awake, but it was before the first hints of sun lit up the sky. Now, light shines in from the blinds. Jasmine has been lying on my chest the entire night, but the pressure of her body isn't enough. I knew she felt it last night, and although I wanted to speak up, I was also still reeling from the rash of feelings that hit me in the chest when I pressed my mouth to hers.

It wasn't planned. I didn't creep into her room as a means to find a place to stick my cock. I didn't even plan on sleeping in her bed, but the pull in this direction was too strong to resist. Truth be told, I needed her. Watching Max walk away from me at the hospital was more painful than I can admit out loud, and I wanted a place to release that anger.

Only it backfired.

The time spent with Jasmine last night has only been matched one other time in my life. It just so happens that the first time I slept with Max is its matching pair. It was sensual and beyond perfect, but at the same time, it wasn't enough. I know Jasmine felt the same way but was also too afraid to speak the truth last night.

Unease must still be in her bones because she's been awake on my chest for the last ten minutes and she hasn't made a single move to pull away. It's awkward and childish, but I'm still giving her a reprieve because I haven't moved either.

After another five minutes of her not speaking, I throw myself on the grenade.

"This doesn't work without him, does it?"

At first, her tears are the only clue that she heard me, and I hold her tighter when a shuddering sob escapes her throat.

"I'm so sorry."

"We should go get him back."

I've spent the better part of the last ten hours trying to talk myself out of returning to Florida and dragging Max right back here. Regardless of his declaration that there isn't anything in New Mexico for him, I have an agonizing need to prove him otherwise. He has me, and he has Jasmine. Everything will fall into place.

"You should get him back," she clarifies. "He's yours, not ours."

She sounds resolved, albeit heartbroken with the declaration.

I push against her until she's up on her elbow and avoiding my gaze. Her cheeks are red, lips trembling, and I can tell she wants to avoid this conversation. Hell, she's been trying to avoid this conversation since the conversation we had in the SUV after her dad walked in on the three of us at the clubhouse. As if she's always known where we were going to end up, she's resolved.

"That's where you're wrong," I tell her. "This doesn't work without you either."

"I'm not going to come in between the two of you."

She says the words with determination like she made her mind up long ago and just now has the strength to speak the decision out loud.

"There is no in between. Not with you and me. Not with him and me, and not with him and you."

"I don't need you to placate me because you're naked in my bed."

I grab her before she can slip away.

"No more fucking running." I soften my words by cupping the side of her neck, so I can sweep my thumb over her cheek. Her eyes flutter, but then a tear rolls down her cheek, and I realize I have a lot more convincing to do.

"This is too painful for me."

"Right now, or when you think that it's going to end?"

Her throat works on a swallow, but she doesn't answer. I don't know if she has an answer.

"Jasmine."

When her eyes find mine, it breaks my heart in two. Words don't seem like the solution. There's a piece of the puzzle that's currently missing, and until all three of us are in the same room so we can hash this mess out, we won't have answers.

So, I do the only thing I can think of; I press my mouth to hers, wondering why I waited so long in the first place. She doesn't take as long to respond to me this time. Last night it was agony while I waited for her to get on the same page as me. This morning she opens her mouth, her tongue seeking mine before I get the chance to look for hers, but it's wrong, and not in the missing sense.

Right now feels exactly like it did with Max outside of the hospital. She isn't kissing me because she needs me, somehow, she's trying to tell me goodbye. Well, I won't fucking have it.

"No," I hiss when I pull my mouth away.

She blinks down at me, her eyes keeping contact with mine when I place both palms on her cheeks.

"Everything will work out, but you need to have faith that it will," I tell her.

She looks away, my grip on her face making it to where she can only pull her eyes far enough away to look at my shoulder.

"Jasmine, I'll spank your ass if you keep this up."

Her breath hitches, but my naughty girl shifts her gaze back to mine.

"We'll bring him home, and until then we'll save everything for when we're back together again."

"Everything?" she whispers as her hips shift so she's straddling me.

"Yes," I assure her.

Knowing that we're going to be working together to get Max back here with us gives me enough strength to keep from sliding into her, but that doesn't mean I have to forgo everything. Her mouth, the press of her lips against mine isn't something I'll ever deprive myself of ever again.

"Last night was the first time you kissed me."

"I know."

"Every time we've hooked up before, you never kissed my lips."

"I know."

"I thought you were avoiding it because it was too personal."

"I was."

Saying it out loud makes me feel like an even bigger asshole, but before recently, our interaction, my interactions with every partner since Max was only about getting off. Sex could be intimate without pressing my mouth to someone else's.

"I shouldn't have waited so long to kiss you."

"I also thought it was a way to distance yourself. Like you had a real issue with giving me that last part of you." I don't have to confess my truth. She already knows it. "I think that's also the reason bottoming for Max was never an option for you. You're unwilling to go all in."

"Max doesn't want me to bottom for him," I assure her. "He's always wanted me inside of him, not the other way around."

"How can you be so sure?" she argues.

"He told me."

"Years and years ago?" I nod. "Don't you think there's a possibility that things have changed for him?"

"I'm not opposed to the idea," I lie. Honestly, I never pictured myself being dominated by anyone, male or female alike.

I can admit that his fingers inside of me, the harsh brush of his digits against my prostate gets me off like nothing else, but being taken? That's never been on my wish list.

"Do you think he really wants to?"

Jasmine shrugs, the action a slight movement with her pressed once again to my bare chest.

"I know I'd love to see it."

I smile at her answer, enthralled that she enjoys the sight of Max and me together.

"I guess we can add that to the list of things to discuss when he gets back."

I feel her lips tug up in a smile against my chest.

"Are there going to be rules?"

"I don't know," I answer honestly. "I've never done this before."

"What exactly is this?" she asks.

My lips curl up into a smile, loving that even though we've agreed to convince Max to come back to us, she can't help acting like a typical woman and asking a million questions she knows I don't have the answer to.

"Why don't we text him and see what we're working with?"

She climbs off the bed, fully naked and uncaring that my eyes track her every movement until she's hiding the milky flesh of her tits and torso with the same t-shirt we discarded last night. I don't bother with clothes and revel in the feel of her eyes on my skin as I walk out of the room to retrieve my cell phone from the jeans I tossed aside last night.

I shoot a text off, but it returns as undeliverable. Giving Jasmine the number, I wait as she sends him a text as well. She gets the same result.

"He's such an asshole," I mutter, setting my phone on the side table near the couch.

I pull her into my arms before reaching for the remote.

"What does it mean?" she asks, her tone soft and disenchanted.

"It means he's a stubborn fool, but that's only going to make it so much sweeter when he's back in New Mexico."

She snuggles closer as I kiss the top of her head. Max staying away forever isn't an option, even if I have to hogtie him and drag him back to the desert.

"We'll give him through the holidays to come to his senses," I tell her as I settle on a police procedural rerun.

"And if he doesn't?"

"Then we track him down and take away every single reason he can think of to keep us at arm's length."

"Will you tell me about what happened in Florida?"

As much as I want to avoid talking about the emotion that bubbled to a head last night in her arms, I know she deserves at least the Cliff Notes' version. I don't want to damage her with the details, but she's going to need to know where Max's head is at with his sister when we get him back home.

Chapter 32

Max

"I figured these would be better than the ones the hospital has given you."

I hold out the fuzzy socks, but Mia doesn't even look at me in acknowledgment, much less reach for them.

"They're your favorite colors," Ma urges. "More pink than turquoise, just how you like."

My sister still doesn't respond, and I'm lost. I don't know what to do or how to make this better.

I'm frustrated with her, and that makes me feel like an asshole. I don't expect her to just blink one day and welcome me back with open arms, but a little sign that she's happy I'm still alive would go a long way.

"Those are perfect," Scooter says as he takes the new pack of socks from my hands.

He doesn't exactly treat her with kids gloves, but he's the only one she'll allow to get close to her.

My parents and I watch as once again, Scooter reaches out to her. With kind words and reassurances, he pulls back the blankets at her feet, pulling the green hospital-issued socks from her feet before replacing them with the ones I tried to offer her. He squeezes each foot before replacing the blankets.

She had another screaming fit a few days ago, but the tears dried up once Scooter came back into the room. He's been here every second since. We don't say what we all know. Eventually, he's going to have to return to his life back in New Mexico, and if we don't start getting her used to him not being around, we're going to have trouble.

A nurse brings in her lunch tray, but she doesn't even look in the woman's direction. One hundred percent of her focus is on Scooter and whatever his next move may be.

"The doctor wants to meet with you in the hall," the nurse says before she walks out.

Scooter doesn't budge from her bedside as my parents and I leave the room to speak with the doctor that has been managing her care for the last seventy-two hours.

"Dr. McCormick," I greet with my hand out as we approach him.

"How is she doing?" my dad asks, but we all know the answer to that.

Jason left yesterday, unable to watch his fiancée with her arms around a man that isn't him. He told us he had some things to take care of back home, needed to clear his schedule a little more, but I doubt the man will be back. He doesn't seem the type to deal with the things Mia will need in the weeks and months ahead. The woman blowing up his phone the last couple of days seemed just as impatient. The man has no backbone. He gave up on my sister within days of her disappearance it seems.

"Physically, Mia is doing very well. She'll have the cast on her arm for several more weeks, but she's healed dramatically over the last couple of days," Dr. McCormick informs us.

We all hear what he isn't saying.

"Her discharge papers will be ready this afternoon."

"Discharge?" my mother asks, distrust clear in her tone. "She isn't ready to be discharged. She hardly eats. She won't look anyone in the eye. She hasn't spoken a word to any of us since she screamed us all out of the room after waking up from surgery."

I'm not the only one my sister has been torturing with her silence. My parents are being punished, too. Although she looks right through me, I've explained more than once that they didn't know about my fake death and my time in the FBI, but that information hasn't made her demeanor change either.

"As I said, physically she's healing. Her emotional recovery will take much more time. There are some outpatient resources—"

"Outpatient?" I hiss. "She's practically catatonic."

I peer behind him into the room to find Scooter spoon-feeding her the soup from her lunch tray.

"If it weren't for that man in there, she would be wasting away," my father states.

The doctor knows how true his words are. He's paid extra attention to my sister since her arrival, and I'm certain it was at the request of Cerberus.

"There is no quick fix, no medication I can give Mia to help her move through the stages of trauma any quicker," Dr. McCormick says with a sigh. "If there was a way for me to help her and the other women, I'd do it in a heartbeat. She has a long road ahead of her. My suggestion would be to ensure that Mr. Nolan is able to stick close by until she's capable of reaching out to others for help."

I begin to pace. "And if we can't? The man has a life to get back to."

"She also has Jason," Ma says, grasping at straws.

"Her fiancé may not be an option. Many victims of trafficking no longer trust the people from their previous lives. They blame their loved ones for not protecting them," the doctor says.

"That's ridiculous," my father snaps. "She was at the mall when she was taken. How could I have protected her from that?"

"It's not always logical. I'm just stating a fact. I don't know if that's what's going on. Just letting you know that it's a common occurrence. Her body is healing, but her mind is still broken."

"Can we postpone her discharge?" Ma asks.

The doctor is shaking his head before she finishes the question. "I'm sorry, but no. We need to open the bed for someone with physical issues that we can treat."

Crestfallen, my mother nods her head in understanding.

"If you follow me, I can give you the information for a couple of places that would be better suited for her long-term care."

I don't join them when my parents walk away. I keep my eyes on my sister. Once vibrant and full of life, she's a shell of herself. It took several years after hearing of my death for her to get back the light in her eyes, but eventually, she was able to smile and laugh. She was able to move on with her life, the proof of that in Jason and her plans to marry.

Now? I don't recognize the broken spirit in the hospital bed. She clings to a man she doesn't know, and that gives me a little hope, but the sparkle is long gone from her eyes. She doesn't smile at him. She hasn't replaced Jason with him. She's a shadow of the person she used to be, and it's been that way since she woke up.

I have no clue how to help her.

I stand in the doorway until she clamps her lips closed, refusing the food on the spoon Scooter offers her. Before long, she's curling into his side and letting her eyes flutter closed. It's long moments before the clenched fist in his shirt relaxes, and he's able to put some distance between the two of them.

I'm not beyond begging him to stay with her. I'd offer him every dime in my bank account if I thought it was enough to convince him to stick around, but I know from the look in his eyes as he climbs off of the bed to walk toward me, that I'm not going to like his answer.

"She has to speak to me eventually," I tell him as I continue to watch her from the doorway.

She hasn't woken yet, but her brow furrowed the second he broke contact with her.

"Give her time to heal," he tells me. The words aren't condescending. He isn't growing frustrated with her inability to let him have some space.

"She's being discharged this afternoon," I inform him.

He sighs. "I figured it was coming soon."

"You already know what I'm going to ask." He nods. "If there was any other way, any other person on this earth who would make her feel safe, I'd have them here in a heartbeat."

"I can't stay in Florida with her."

"My parents are going back to Louisiana, I imagine."

"I have to return to New Mexico."

Even though I knew it was coming, the words from his mouth hit me in the chest like a ten-ton brick.

Christmas music plays softly overhead, and even though it's Christmas Day, the last thing any of us feel like doing is celebrating the holiday. It should be a time of happiness and rejoicing, yet here we stand watching a broken woman sleep restlessly in a hospital bed.

"I'm afraid she'll hurt herself if you're not around," I confess.

I've heard the stories. I've spent the last couple of days researching the best ways to help her move on from this, only to be slapped in the face with the reality that some women don't.

"I don't think she'll do that."

"Even if she doesn't intentionally injure herself, refusing to eat will do exactly that."

We continue to watch her, and it kills me that I can't be that person for her, just as I know it guts my father and Jason alike for not being the ones she reached out to in her pain.

Helpless doesn't even begin to describe how we all feel.

"I want to kill every single one of them," I mumble.

"We will," he assures me.

Mia starts to whimper in her sleep, and Scooter goes to her immediately. He doesn't sigh or seem frustrated at his duties as he climbs back in her bed, draws her against his chest, and wraps his protective arms around her.

As much as I want to gear up and head straight to fucking Venezuela on a suicide mission, I know that I'm needed here. Even though my sister wants nothing to do with me, I pray that eventually she'll wake up one day and her family members are the ones she's reaching for.

Chapter 33

Jasmine

"How many more days?" I ask him.

"Two not counting today," Kingston answers, his voice just as weary as mine.

It's New Year's Eve, but neither one of us feel like doing anything other than watching TV.

Christmas was exhausting, having been spent with my family. We were both walking on eggshells around my dad and Uncle Diego.

I was floored when Kingston confessed that he was invited by both of them. I don't think they've accepted my choice in lifestyle, but maybe they're coming around to the fact that I'm going to live my life like I want to. What I'm doing doesn't hurt anyone, unless you count Kingston and me, who've been aching for Max for the last week.

The time we spend together has been amazing, but there's a gap in our lives in the shape of one stubborn Hispanic man. We decided that he must've tossed his old phone or deactivated it or something because each message and attempt to call was rejected. Kingston spoke with Scooter the day after arriving back in New Mexico, and he let us know that Max, as well as his parents, were still at the hospital with Mia.

"I feel like we should be doing something," I whisper.

"What do you mean?"

"Like we should be actively trying to get him back."

"We need to give him time."

"You didn't give me time," I argue. "You crawled into my bed after breaking into my apartment."

"I didn't break into your apartment. I have a key."

"A key you made without permission," I remind him. "I told you I wanted it back."

"It was never yours, to begin with."

"Because you obtained it through ill-gotten means."

He laughs, low and husky, and I love the vibrations against my cheek as I lay my head on his lap.

My phone chirps, but I don't bother to move. I can't focus on the TV, and honestly, I haven't been able to focus on much of anything. I haven't done much over the last week, but exhaustion has somehow settled in my bones.

Kingston's phone chirps next, but unlike me, he shifts so he can pull his from his pocket.

"Don't respond to that," I mutter as the light from his phone lights up the living room.

"It's your dad," he says.

"Even more reason."

"He's inviting us to the party at the clubhouse."

"Decline," I urge him.

Before Kingston can type out a message, his phone chirps again. Instead of reading it off to me, he turns the phone so I can read the message.

"Crap," I hiss.

Dad isn't inviting us; rather he's insisting that we show up.

Proof of life, the text message reads since no one has seen me since we left after Christmas lunch.

"I'll just call him," I tell Kingston, making no move to get off his lap.

"Let's go."

He urges me to sit up, but I grumble the entire way.

"I don't want to go."

"Neither do I, but I'm also not going to get off on the wrong foot with your family."

"We got off on the wrong foot when he caught me sucking two dicks," I remind him.

He glares at me, but I just shrug.

"Fine, but I'm not dressing up. They can take me how I come or not at all."

"At least put a bra on," he says with his eyes laser-focused to the front of my tank top.

"I thought you liked me like this." I pull my shoulders back, sticking my tits out further.

I'm wound like a top. We've kissed until our lips are raw, but the unspoken rule is that we don't go any further until Max is with us.

"I love you like this." His finger trails down my nipple, causing goosebumps to flash down my arm. "But I don't want the other guys seeing what's Max's and mine."

Isn't it crazy how this man can share me with Max, let me play with others at the club in Denver, but he's possessive of letting the other Cerberus members even getting to see the outline of my nipple?

"Go on," he urges, and as much as I want to torture him by running my hand up his thigh to the erection already straining in his jeans, I refrain.

He also convinced me to wash my face, brush my hair, and throw on a dress, but that's all the effort I put into tonight. Thirty minutes later, we're pulling into the lot at Cerberus. I'm already tired, and it's only late evening. We still have several hours until the ball drops.

"We don't have to stay until midnight," I tell him as he opens my door, so I can climb out of the SUV.

"Let's play it by ear."

"I'm so tired," I complain, but he takes my hand and leads me to the front, anyway.

"You're tired because you've been a bump on a log for the last week."

"You haven't been much better," I grumble, but plaster a fake smile on my face when we walk inside.

Explaining to anyone why we're both kind of over being around people isn't an option tonight.

"Do you think your dad is going to say something about me living with you?" Kingston asks as we make our way across the living room.

I squeeze his hand tighter, forcing him to look down at me. "No, because you aren't living with me."

"Aren't I?" he challenges. "I haven't slept apart from you since I got back from Florida."

"You're an extended houseguest," I clarify.

"So, you want me to stay here tonight?"

"No," my answer is a whisper. Just the thought of going home alone makes my heart race, and not in a good way.

"It's about time you got here!"

I turn just in time for Delilah to wrap her arms around me.

"How's married life?" I ask when she finally releases me so I can breathe again.

"Tug," Lawson says as he catches up with his wife.

The guys shake hands, and I already know where the night is going to go when Delilah looks from me to Kingston and back again. I'm certain all the little gossips here have filled them in on what happened at their wedding reception. Other than the one conversation I had with the group while the guys were in Florida, I haven't spoken to anyone. We stuck to mundane things for our holiday meal since all the parents were around, and I'm glad because I'm stuck in limbo right now waiting for Max to join us, so we can actually discuss what our futures look like.

"So?" Delilah clasps my arms, leaving Lawson to speak with Tug as she drags me to the other side of the room where all the girls are clustered together.

"Good to see you, baby girl," my dad says with a quick kiss to my temple before he walks toward Kingston.

"He's a sitting duck," Sophia says as Delilah drags me down to sit beside her on one of the sofas. "If he can't go head to head with Dad, then you don't need him in your life."

We all watch the two men talk. I don't know what they're saying, but Lawson looks a little uncomfortable standing there as the odd man out. He smiles in the direction of his bride when he locates her, and then everything seems right in his world.

"So, are you two together?" Delilah asks.

"Of course, they are," Ivy assures her friend. "Didn't you see them walking in hand in hand?"

"Because hand-holding is the epitome of a relationship," Gigi mutters.

"They've been together every moment for the last week," Sophia adds.

"How do you know?" I ask my sister.

"I heard Mom and Dad talking about it. You wouldn't believe the things I heard them assuming you were doing with your Christmas break."

My cheeks heat. "Well, they'd be wrong."

We made love the first night he returned from Florida, but we've managed to keep things mostly PG since then, although I'm not going to explain any of that to them.

"Here."

I look up to see Camryn holding out a glass for me.

"What is it?" I ask but take the glass from her hand anyway.

"I don't know, but it's strong."

I lift it in mock salute before throwing the contents down my throat. It burns all the way down, and I hiss through the pain.

"Wow," Gigi mutters. "Maybe there is trouble in paradise."

"We can change the conversation, or I'm going to go hang out with the parents," I tell the group.

Each of them frowns. Well, all except for Griffin who is distracted by Ivy as she sits in his lap. He whispers things in her ear that is enough to make her blush.

My eyes find Kingston. He's talking with Scooter and Rocker, but my hackles rise when his face grows angry. A second later he's shoving past his friend and disappearing down the hallway leading to his room.

Chapter 34

Tug

I didn't have a problem with Delilah dragging Jasmine away until her father stepped up to talk to me. We haven't really had a conversation other than small talk since he found us at the wedding reception. Although I don't imagine we'll talk directly about that night; I pray we get to a point where he isn't glaring at me like I corrupted his child.

"That was intense," Scooter says when Dominic finally walks away.

The conversation was simple, discussing the plans we have to head back to South America, but there's still a ton of tension between us.

"How's Mia?" I ask my friend when we're standing alone.

"About the same."

"I never thought she'd let you walk away from her."

The way she clung to him was concerning, but it sometimes happens, especially to the guys first on the scene.

"She didn't."

I frown at his words.

"What's that supposed to mean?"

He looks around the room before answering, "She's here."

His words are a whisper, like a secret he doesn't want anyone to know.

"She's here?"

I look around the room, but the woman I've always seen as a little sister is nowhere to be found.

"She's in my room."

"No shit? I can't imagine that went over well with her parents and Max."

"It didn't," he huffs. "I can barely get the man out of my room long enough to get some sleep myself."

"What?" He's not making any sense. "Max is here?"

He nods.

"How long has he been here?"

There's no way Max is back in New Mexico. If he came back, he would've sought me out. Or at least shown up at Jasmine's apartment. Right?

"We came back Christmas Day."

"A week?" I hiss.

I don't give him time to answer. I storm away from him and hit the hallway to his room. Mia is asleep on his bed, still bruised and broken like when I left the hospital. Max is napping in the chair in the corner, but his dark head snaps up.

"Are you fucking kidding me?" I snap when his eyes meet mine. "You're here?"

"Don't wake her." He stands from the chair, and my fists clench with the urge to pop him in his damn nose. "We can talk in the hall."

"I think we're going to need a little more privacy than that," I counter, grabbing him by the front of his t-shirt and pushing him into my room a couple of doors down.

"I don't have a fucking clue where this anger and hostility is coming from, but you need to lay off." He shoves me away, his hands raking over the top of his head.

"You don't have a clue? Are you purposely trying to hurt us?"

"Us?" Confusion draws his brows in. "I'm here to make sure my sister is safe."

"There isn't another place on earth that she'd be safer. You've been here a damn week, and not once have you come to see us?"

"What's with this *us* you're jabbering about."

I freeze. "You may not want to see me, but I find it hard to believe you haven't gone once to see Jasmine."

At least he looks a little guilty.

"Mia is my priority."

I nod my head understanding where he's coming from, but at the same time getting angrier by the second. We've been miserable this last week without him. How could he be so close and not want to reach out to us for comfort?

"Is it so easy for you to forget about me? Forget about Jasmine?"

"I haven't forgotten." He sighs before plopping down on my bed like his legs are no longer strong enough to support his weight. "You don't need me."

"The hell we don't. You turned your phone off. We've been trying to get a hold of you for days."

"Out of guilt. You two don't need me."

"We don't work without you."

"Then maybe you aren't compatible after all."

"Kingston?"

We both turn our heads when my bedroom door opens, and Jasmine sticks her head in.

"Max?" she squeals before shoving the door completely open, so she can run across the room to him.

Without warning, she throws herself into his arms. Contrary to what he just said to me, he wraps his arms all the way around her, burying his nose in her hair. Her back shakes with sobs, and I want to kick him for being right under our noses while we've spent excruciating days without him.

We both deserve better than what he's made us suffer through, but even with that thought, I take a step back and assess what he's been through this last week as well. On top of coming back from the dead, he's had to endure his sister and the pain she's going through. Although it hurts to realize we weren't his first thought, I understand where the man is coming from.

"Don't cry, sweet girl," Max coos in Jasmine's ear.

"You're really here?" she says after a long moment of clinging to him.

"I'm here."

"How long?" Jasmine looks over her shoulder at me, her hand reaching out to invite me into the embrace. "Was this a surprise?"

I don't want to lie to the woman, but I also don't want to hurt her and make her feel the same things I'm feeling.

"Max had to get some things straightened out," I tell her instead.

"I'm so glad you're back," she whispers, burying her face in his throat once again.

His eyes find mine over her shoulder, and I don't know if he's grateful I covered for him or angry I didn't tell her the exact truth.

"We've been waiting for you," she tells him just before pressing her mouth to his.

As angry as I am, my cock jerks in my jeans at the sight of them kissing. Max doesn't hold back like I thought he would, and it's clear that Jasmine is the glue holding us both together.

"God, I've missed you," she whispers when his mouth finds her neck.

The grip of his hand in her hair to hold her at the perfect angle for his assault makes my hands itch to do the same to both of them, but I keep my distance. With the heat running through my veins, I want to punish him. Doing so will get us nowhere, however, so I stick to watching.

Jasmine shifts on his hips, doing everything she can to eliminate the distance between them.

"Missed you, too," he confesses as he cups one breast in his large palm while pulling her closer with his other arm at her back.

"Kingston?" Jasmine looks over her shoulder, once again motioning for me to join them.

"I don't think this is the best place for this to happen."

It's like I've poured ice water on both of them. Her hips stop moving, and he releases his grip on her hair.

"Good point," Jasmine says as she tries to move off Max's lap. "We should go back to my apartment."

"I can't leave," Max tells her. "Mia is here."

Jasmine swallows, her hands moving to cover her mouth. "Oh, God, Max. I'm so selfish. I didn't even ask you about your sister."

"It's okay." He smooths down her hair before pressing his lips to her cheek.

"How is she? I'd love to meet her."

"She isn't up for visitors just yet."

Max's eyes find mine once again, and I fully understand what he won't tell her. Mia may never be up for visitors.

Things are worse than I thought. No matter how strong of a woman Mia was before, she's broken right now, and she'll be broken for a long time to come.

"We can stay here," Jasmine assures both of us with a smile. "As long as you need. I'm just happy that we're all together again."

Without another word, I cross the room and lock the door. It won't keep people from knocking, but it will give us a little warning before we're truly interrupted. I don't think sex is the direction the night is going, but I want to cover all of our bases.

Jasmine reaches for the hem of Max's shirt, and he allows her to lift it over his head. When she reaches for the waistband of his sweats, he leans back to give her better access.

Without flare, I strip myself to my boxers before turning off the overhead light, opting to switch on the bedside lamp instead. Jasmine reaches for me when I get close enough to touch them, but I give Max his space. Our girl lifts her mouth to mine, and I feel the heat of his stare on our lips until she pulls away. Unable to resist any longer, I press my mouth to his. He doesn't kiss me back at first, but eventually, he opens his mouth and grants me entrance.

I try to put every ounce of my emotions into the kiss, but it's a sad substitute for the conversation we need to have. I can tell he's distant, but what Max doesn't know is I'm not taking no for an answer. We'll figure everything out, but we need to be a united front to be successful. We have enough passion to power the world, but the commitment is what I'm dying for from him. I know Jasmine feels the same way. We've talked about it, danced around the subject numerous times the last week.

"I fucking missed you," I confess into his mouth.

I expect his hand to reach into my hair. I expect him to force me to my knees so I can take his cock in my mouth, but that doesn't happen.

A strangled sob escapes his lips. I wrap my arms around him as Jasmine climbs from his lap. She strips to her panties as I lay Max down on the bed, positioning him against my chest. Our girl flicks the lamp off before climbing on the opposite side and curling up against his back. We cocoon him with our bodies, lending him the strength he needs until he's able to find it again himself.

"Not going to be a problem," Jasmine responds as her arm reaches back and she grips the meat of Kingston's ass in her hand. I clasp my fingers on top of hers and squeeze as she begins to shake.

"Ohhh," she moans. The one word drags out so long, marking her pleasure that it seems the length of a sonnet.

"That's it," Kingston praises, and I hate that I'm missing the grasp of her cunt on my own cock as she comes, but Kingston doesn't disappoint. He's the next to find his release, and the pulse of his prostate against my dick is nothing short of spectacular.

"Fuck that's good," I tell him, my hips taking over the thrusting.

He groans when my cock jerks inside of him, kicking repeatedly with my own release.

We don't move, laying there long enough for the sweat on our skin to dry.

Chapter 36

Jasmine

"Well, this is messy," Kingston complains when he shifts his weight.

He's the first one to climb out of bed, but if it were up to me, we'd never leave.

Max laughs as he watches Kingston shuffle to the bathroom. I stare, too, but there isn't anything funny about the way his back muscles ripple under his golden skin.

"Do I have you to thank for this?" Max asks me.

I turn over on the mattress to face him, shifting my body to close the distance between us. My overheated skin prickles with the contact.

"What do you have to thank me for?"

"He would've never let me do that to him if he hadn't been persuaded."

"He told me once you never wanted to fuck him. He claimed that you preferred the bottom."

"I normally do," he says with an easy grin. "But I may have found my new favorite thing."

His eyes light up, and I realize it's exactly what was missing last night when I came in here to discover that he was at Cerberus. His true happiness didn't shine last night. This morning, it's still clouded with demons.

"Good luck convincing him to do that every single time."

He chuckles, but the sound is forced.

"I want to—"

"I hate showering alone!" Kingston yells from the bathroom. "Both of you get in here."

"He's a demanding man, isn't he?" I ask but move to get off the bed.

Max follows, but it's clear when we step into the bathroom that there isn't even close to enough room in the shower for all three of us.

"You first," I urge as Max looks between me and the shower. "This is one of my fantasies playing out."

He looks apprehensive at first, but the soap bubbles traveling down Kingston's muscular thighs would be enough to entice a nun into the shower with him. Max steps inside and Kingston's hands immediately go to work. I don't know if they're purposely putting on a show when their hands skate over each other's bodies, but my reaction is the same. Even after the powerful orgasm I just had, my desire is renewed at the sight of them. Since I've decided to no longer hide my appetite for these men, I do the only thing I can think of in this moment. I sit on the toilet seat, leaning my back against the wall, and let my fingers trace the lips of my sex. They don't notice me immediately, too caught up in their own pleasure, but when they do, I become their pleasure.

"You don't have any idea how sexy you are with his cum dripping from you," Max says as his own hand begins to stroke his dick.

"Why don't you taste her," Kingston urges.

My body trembles at the concept of Max licking away what Kingston left behind.

It's all he has to say before Max steps out of the shower and lowers his mouth to my aching pussy. At first, his only focus is to lick Kingston's essence from my skin, but eventually, his tongue finds my clit.

"That's so fucking hot," Kingston praises as he jacks his own dick.

"I've missed this pussy," Max says as he works me even faster. "Missed you."

His words make the back of my eyes burn from tears. We haven't had the chance to talk, but I hope that his confession means he's willing to make things work with the three of us. We're built on a foundation of sexual pleasure, but stronger relationships have been built on less.

I don't have the ability to focus on that, however, because his mouth goes into overdrive the same time his fingers push inside of me, and I'm lost to him. Lost to his mouth and lost to Kingston as he smiles at the two of us. My orgasm isn't as powerful as the one I had before, but it's just as pleasurable, leaving me satiated and replete.

"Get in here and rinse off," Kingston tells Max when he pulls his mouth away only to kiss the inside of both my thighs. "Then it's Jasmine's turn. We can spend the next month in bed together, but there's a conversation we have to have first."

Anxiety swims in my gut with his declaration. I've had boyfriends, of course, but honestly, I could take them or leave them. They always had an expiration date, a moment when the desire and feelings changed that left nothing but the choice to walk away. Convincing two people to stick together is hard enough. Three seems damn near impossible. There're so many factors, so many things to consider, an extra person to take care of, more needs to be met to keep everyone happy. From the outside looking in, it seems impossible.

"Look at me," Kingston urges with his finger crooked under my chin as I step into the shower.

My mouth waters with the need to speak, to confess all of my doubts, but the flood of words never come. Instead, I give him a weak smile and allow him to wash away the sex and sweat from my body.

By the time we climb out of the shower and dry off, Max is gone from the room. My apprehension is compounded as I look to Kingston to see his jaw working. He told Max we needed to talk, but it seems the man was all too eager to disappear.

"Where do you think he went?" I ask as I begrudgingly pull on my clothes from last night sans panties.

Kingston doesn't answer, but his eyes track my movements as I shift my dress into place.

"We need to find him and get back to your apartment. I don't want you walking around the clubhouse without something covering my pretty little pussy."

My eyes roll as I slip into my shoes. The man is willing to share me with Max, but just the thought of another man seeing what's beneath my clothes turns him into a jealous monster.

"Your pussy?"

"Mine and Max's," he clarifies.

"I'm not so sure everyone is on the same page." I don't specify Max because I'm not so sure Kingston and I are on the same page either.

We've held off, refusing to speak about the future while waiting for the holidays to end so we could seek Max out, and even though he's hinted at a future with the three of us together, he hasn't just come out and said that's what he's wanting.

"We'll get there." His words are sure, a promise that things will be okay.

I want to ask him where he's getting his confidence from, but a whispered argument in the hall draws both of our attention.

"I said she's sleeping."

I recognize the voice as Scooter's when Kingston opens the bedroom door, and we step into the hallway.

An angry Max is standing with fists clenched as he squares up with the other Cerberus man.

"I want to see her."

"Nothing has changed in the last seven hours, Max. Let her rest," Scooter insists.

A female whimper meets my ears, but in the darkness surrounding us, I can't see past Scooter into his room. He looks agitated when he looks over his shoulder, but I can't tell if he's annoyed with Max's interruption or whoever is in his room.

"Why is she upset?" Max questions.

"Because she's fitful when I leave," Scooter answers. "Let me get back to her."

"This isn't healthy," Max says, but he seems resigned. The anger has drained from his body, leaving him slightly slumped and defeated. "She needs to face what's happened, so she can begin to heal."

"And she'll do that when she's ready."

"She won't ever be ready if you continue to coddle her. You're only letting her get lost in her head."

The whimpering grows louder, and without a word, Scooter steps back and closes the door in Max's face.

"Who's in there?" I ask Kingston, but I have a feeling I already know the answer.

Max told me last night that Mia was in the clubhouse, but it doesn't make any sense to me that she'd be in Scooter's room.

"Max," Kingston says as he reaches his hand out for his friend, "let her rest."

"She's done nothing but rest for the better part of two weeks."

"And we'll let her continue for a month if that's what she needs. She's in good hands, and from her reaction to him, this is exactly what she needs right now."

Head hung low, Max walks past him into one of the guest bedrooms down the hall. I'm unsure if we should follow him, but when Kingston heads that way, I follow.

"We need to talk," Kingston tells him as we both step inside of the room.

Max is stripping off the sweats and t-shirt that he put back on after his shower, but there isn't anything sensual about his actions. He merely picks up another t-shirt from an open suitcase in the closet and pulls it over his head before grabbing a pair of jeans and donning those as well.

"Then talk," Max says after a long moment.

"I don't think this is the best place," Kingston observes.

I don't add that this really isn't the right time. Max is agitated, and the topic of conversation is too important and serious to have while he isn't in the right frame of mind. I consider seducing him, getting him sexed-up until he's a little more amenable, but I wouldn't want to be manipulated that way, so I won't do the same to him.

"Let's go back to Jasmine's apartment," Kingston urges, but it's clear by the look on Max's face that he's no more willing to leave the clubhouse now than he was last night.

"Whatever needs to be said, can be said right here," Max says with a huff before sitting on the bed and crossing his arms over his chest like a petulant child that's about to get dressed down by a parent.

This isn't how I wanted this to go at all.

Chapter 37

Max

Maybe it's for the best that Kingston is going to tell me that he and Jasmine have decided to give their relationship a go. I have a million other things going on and focusing on the two of them will only be an added distraction I don't need. It doesn't stop the dread deep in my stomach, though.

They may want to fuck me, may want to add me into their sex lives for a little spice every once in a while, but eventually, I'll be discarded just like the last time Kingston saw something more promising on the horizon.

Kingston's eyes dart to Jasmine, and although pain fills his face, I know what's coming. His hands scrape over the top of his head, and I can tell that he's not taking any pleasure in what he's about to say, even though he won't let that stop him.

"I don't even know where to begin," he muses.

"I can go first," Jasmine says as she takes another step into the room.

Kingston nods, taking the pussy way out as he steps around her to close the bedroom door.

"I really like…" she says to me, and for some reason, I take both of her hands when she offers them to me. "Really like both of you."

She tosses a quick look back over her shoulder. Kingston gives her a quick smile but doesn't encourage her to say more.

"I just…" she begins, but when she looks back at me, her eyes glisten with tears.

I cup her jaw, letting my thumb run down her cheek. I shouldn't be comforting her. I shouldn't be making it easier to walk away from me, but I can't help myself. She's an amazing woman, one of the most beautiful women I've had the pleasure of meeting and walking away from her is going to hurt more than I ever imagined.

"It's okay," I assure her. "I understand."

And I do, to a point. I'm all too aware of the draw Kingston demands just by existing, how easy it is to become enamored by him, to crave his affection like a drug. I went thirteen years without a fix, and it only took one shot, one look in his stormy eyes and I was once again relapsing back into his orbit.

The surprise is *her*. Jasmine tugs at me the very same way Kingston does, but the shocking need will be over soon enough.

"You do?" Jasmine asks.

"I do. I know how easy it is to fall for him."

I don't let my eyes roam to Kingston, the agony of losing him is already seeping in, and the last thing I want to do is let him know how much he still affects me.

She smiles down at me conspiratorially like we're sharing a secret that isn't obvious to anyone else.

"I didn't mean for it to happen," she confesses, and I can see the truth in her smile.

She's been fooled just like I have been, but instead of warning her away, instead of reminding her that he'll walk away from her just as he's planning to walk away from me now, I can't get my lips to move. While Kingston is around, he's the most amazing thing the world has to offer. It's the part when he leaves that's the true bitch. I won't deny her the time with him.

"And imagine my surprise when I realized I feel the same for you."

My head tilts. *Did she just say—*

"Don't look so shocked," Kingston says as he walks up behind her and places his hand at her back. "And while she's confessing, I have disclosures to make as well."

"What?" It's the only word I can manage right now. This isn't going where I expected it to go at all.

"We want to be together," Kingston says. "I want to be with you and her."

"I want to be with you and him," Jasmine adds.

"What?" Still, nothing is computing.

"The three of us," Kingston clarifies. "Together. Me with you and her, and her with me and you. You with both of us."

His eyebrows shoot up like facial expressions will help me understand easier.

"I thought you guys were here to tell me that you'd decided I was the third wheel, and you wanted to let me know."

Jasmine's hand goes to her throat, and right in that second, it's abundantly clear that this was never their intention. "What gave you that idea?"

"I just thought—"

"Still haven't gotten rid of that self-esteem issue, I see," Kingston grunts. "You're going to have to work on that."

My jaw clenches with the need to shove him to the floor and show him just how strong my self-esteem is with a couple of blows to his face, but he's actually right on the money with his assessment.

"D-Do you not want the same?" Jasmine's lower lip trembles, and it makes me want to kiss her pain away.

My heart is pounding behind my rib cage, and I can only imagine the trauma this one-hundred-and-eighty-degree turn of events is causing my body.

"Together?" My eyes dart between the two of them. "You both want all three of us together?"

The tears threatening to fall from Jasmine's lashes finally crest, and the sight of her doubt running down her face is enough to destroy me. It makes me realize that I'd do anything in this world to keep her from feeling pain, and somehow that's just as strong as the love I've always felt for Kingston Jacks.

"Shhh," I purr, wiping at her tears with the tip of my finger. "Don't cry, sweet girl."

"Can you answer the damn question?" the ever impatient Kingston mutters.

Having known me for so long, no matter the distance, he's still more than capable of reading my thoughts long before they leave my lips, but after the near heartbreak I just suffered, I plan to make him sweat it out.

When I lower my head to collect my thoughts, I don't miss the straining erection in his jeans. He knows what my response will be, and he's already gearing up to celebrate. My own cock stiffens with anticipation, and my mouth waters for him to fuck my throat. Add in Jasmine, and we've got one combustible combination that I may never get enough of.

The only problem is I can't be selfish. I can't let the lure of them and their promises of not only sexual fulfillment but the perfection of having the emotional side of them as well lead me astray. I'm in New Mexico for my sister, and as appealing as the bonus of the two of them while I'm here is, I know my stay will eventually come to an end. Being selfish right now will only hurt everyone in the end.

"This will never work," I tell them when I lift my head to look at them.

"Not funny," Kingston spits. "This isn't the time for jokes."

Jasmine freezes, standing stock still, the tremble in her hands the only clue that she's reacting to what I said.

"Starting something with the two of you—"

"This started long before now," Kingston interrupts.

"When Mia is ready, we'll be leaving New Mexico," I remind him.

"You don't have to go. We can find a way to make this work."

"Please?" Jasmine begs, and it kills me to see new tears flooding her eyes.

"It's not possi—"

A knock at the door seals my lips.

"Max, we still need—" Dominic opens the door and sticks his head inside, but the sight of his daughter once again alone with two men narrows his eyes. They flare with anger when Jasmine turns to face him, and he sees the tears on her face. "I don't like seeing you cry, baby girl."

The warning is clear in his tone, and I'm sure he's ready to kill us both when she takes in a shuddering breath.

"I'd ask you to explain," Dominic begins, "but all of you are grown. I'm here if you need me."

The last part is meant for his daughter, but I can read between the lines. The man would be willing to do whatever she wanted, dole out whatever punishment she can think of for me hurting her. I'd deserve every bit of it, but I also know that hurting them now will be less painful than if I allowed this relationship to grow only to leave later.

"I hate to interrupt," Dominic says with his eyes back on me, "but we still have those maps and shipments to go over."

Kingston turns back in my direction, accusation in his cold glare. I've been lending a hand to Cerberus since I came back from Florida. Mia sleeps a lot, and their normal logistics guy Blade has undergone some type of procedure that's left him incapable of working.

"Sure thing," I answer him as I stand from the bed. "Be right there." Dominic nods before stepping back and pulling the door closed.

"I don't fucking think so," Kingston spits as I stand and try to walk past him. "You're not leaving until we talk about this."

"We've already talked about it," I remind him. "You guys made an offer, and I turned it down."

I hate the mocking tone of my voice, but it's the only shield I have for the pain inside of me.

"And it's just that easy for you?" He grips my arm at my elbow, but I welcome the pain. It's a tangible distraction from the gut-wrenching agony in my heart.

"I have to go." I rip my arm from his grasp and walk out of the room.

My own eyes burn with tears when I hear Jasmine begin to sob.

Chapter 38

Tug

"H-he s-said n-no," Jasmine sobs.

Each tear that drenches my shirt, each painful cry from her lips makes me want to tear him apart.

"He didn't," I assure her.

His eyes spoke his truth even as his mouth told his lies. I know Max. I've known him for longer than I've known everyone else in my life short of my abusive father. He could never lie to me, although he's tried a hundred times.

"I heard him. He doesn't want to be with us."

She clings to me tighter, as if she's afraid I'm going to let go of her. What she doesn't know is I won't take his lies at face value. I won't let him walk away from us with the flimsy excuse about leaving town. If I have to persuade his family to uproot and move to New Mexico, I'll move mountains before I let him leave us. He doesn't get to walk back into my life after being dead for so many years only to leave me again. I won't allow it.

"He's focused on Mia and her recovery."

"As he should be."

I hold her tighter. This woman's capacity for selflessness astounds me every day. She will be the glue that holds us all together; now, I just have to figure out a way to ensure that happens.

"Let me talk to him."

Her head is shaking before I can finish my thought.

"We need to do everything together. We have to be united."

While I agree with her, I know what it may take to convince the bastard that our plan is the best one. I don't imagine she'll be too thrilled with the techniques I may have to deploy for that to happen. I recall her cringing in the airplane hangar when I punched him, and it may take more of that to make him see the light.

"We should go. We need to give him a little space," I tell her as I stand from the bed and encourage her to stand.

"I don't want to leave him," she whispers.

"I don't either, but we won't get anywhere by being underfoot. It will only agitate him and make him dig in his heels. I know Max. Let him think about what he's turning down. He'll come around."

"And if he doesn't?"

"I won't let that happen," I assure her as I guide her out of his room.

Several people look at us when we walk through the living room, and I'm sure they all want to know why she's crying and why her bloodshot eyes lower when we walk past. She doesn't want to speak to them, so I hold her tighter against my side and walk her right out the front door without a word to anyone.

The ride back to her apartment is quiet, both of us thinking about Max's rejection. I refuse to focus on what it would mean if he sticks to his guns and continues to reject a relationship with the two of us. I don't know that Jasmine and I would work together alone, but I'm willing to try, even with the heartbreaking loss of Max.

My fingers grip the steering wheel until my knuckles turn white. I'm beyond pissed, beyond wanting to evaluate the reasons for him hurting us.

When Jasmine's hand finds my thigh, I give her a quick glance. A small, sad smile only pulls up one corner of her pretty mouth, and I know she's the one trying to calm me, trying to reassure me that things will work out exactly how they're supposed to.

By the time we make it inside of her apartment, exhaustion has once again settled in my bones. With my past and my childhood as it was, I learned early on that in order to keep the will to go on, I must fight the feelings in my chest. Depression would be so easy to settle into, but once again, I refuse to let it grab hold. Although if I think about it, we've both been depressed to a point the last couple of weeks. Max is an integral part of what we are, and without him, nothing makes sense.

"Happy New Year," Jasmine says, brushing a quick kiss to my lips.

With discovering Max at the clubhouse, I'd forgotten that it even was a holiday. We were all asleep before the clock even got close to striking midnight, but if today is any indication of how the year will be, I want a do-over.

"I'm so tired," Jasmine whines as she beelines for the sofa.

Before she can drop down on the cushion, I grab her shoulders and turn her to face me.

"Let's go do something," I urge.

"Like what?" She doesn't sound the least bit enthused by the suggestion.

"I don't know." My shoulder hitches. "We could go for a bike ride."

That would mean going back to Cerberus to get my bike, and the draw to go after Max would be too strong.

"It's too cold outside." She shivers as if just the thought makes ice form in her blood.

"We could go shopping," I offer.

"I hate shopping, and the after-Christmas masses will be out in droves. No thanks."

"We could go to that diner you like and have a late breakfast."

"I'm not hungry," she argues.

"Yet, you haven't eaten since breakfast yesterday. Come on. Get changed and let's go eat."

She huffs, but thankfully, she heads to the bedroom. I follow her, needing to get out of the clothes I wore yesterday as well, but I find her just standing in her closet staring at her clothes like she's never seen them before.

"We can't focus on what we have right now."

I walk up behind her and press my lips to the back of her head. She leans her weight against my chest, and I wrap my arms around her middle. She's utter perfection in my arms, so we just stand there for a few long moments while we embrace. I need to fix this for her. I need to fix this for myself. I can't get the look in Max's eyes out of my head. He was right there, ready to accept what we were offering, but he backed out at the last minute. It's just part of who he is. Max has always put others before him. He put his family before him instead of going into the Marine Corps with me. We could've left our small town together and been happy, but his dad relied on him. His path was chosen long before he had the ability to make a choice himself. Selflessly, he gave me up to live up to his legacy. Only he gave that up too, spending the last ten years in the FBI instead of walking the path his dad wanted.

He's doing the exact same thing again. He's planning his future based on the rocky assumption that his sister will get better and want to go back to her old life.

"We should lie down," Jasmine whispers.

"Nope." I snap into action, pulling a heavy sweater and a pair of jeans from the hangers to hand to her. "We're going to breakfast."

"And if I refuse?" She turns to face me, her small hand resting against my chest.

"Then I'll spank your ass until you get dressed."

A weak smile crosses her face, but it doesn't reach her eyes. I ignore the pain because there isn't a thing I can do about it this second and move past her to get my own clothes.

I watch her change with appreciative eyes but resist the urge to trail my fingers down the soft skin on her stomach. If I have anything to do with the outcome, I'll have years and years of being able to do just that; only she'll have four hands on her flesh instead of just two.

Five minutes later, we're back outside of her apartment complex and climbing into the SUV. The diner we've been to a handful of times over the last month is warm, the air thick with the scent of sugar and bacon.

"I told you," I mock when Jasmine turns her nose up to take in the scents of breakfast.

She grins, seeming to get out of her head long enough to enjoy my taunting.

"I want one of everything," she says as the waitress gets us settled into a booth.

"Let's start with coffee," I barter as I hand her a menu.

The waitress nods before walking away.

"You loved the French toast the last time we were here, but you weren't too fond of the sausage links," I remind her.

She's frowning when I look up from my menu.

"What's wrong?"

"Everything," she whispers. "Are we just going to make small talk about breakfast with everything that's going on?"

I open my mouth to reassure her, but there's even more going on than she knows. Cerberus leaves tomorrow to head back to Venezuela, and I doubt we'll get to the bottom of anything between now and then. We're on a mission to take down Jiménez and Cortez and seeing as how Cerberus has raided the Cortez compounds twice now with minimal luck, I imagine we'll be gone for a while. It could be weeks before we return, and by that time there's a very good chance Max and Mia will be gone. No matter how dependent on Scooter Mia is, he's not going to turn down the opportunity for blood. He wants vengeance on the men who've been operating with impunity just as much as the rest of us.

"I'm going to get the crepes this time," I smile at her even though she's still frowning at me, "with bananas *and* strawberries."

She shakes her head, frustrated that I won't let her drive the conversation, but when the food is delivered, she digs in and doesn't mention Max again for the next twenty minutes.

Chapter 39

Jasmine

Breakfast begins to sour in my stomach the second we leave the diner. By the time we make it back to my apartment parking lot, I'm sure I won't be able to keep it down.

"I feel like we should be doing something," I tell Kingston as he shifts the SUV into park. "Waiting has never been easy for me."

He chuckles, but the sound is forced. He's not a patient man either.

"We can go to the clubhouse and drag him out. I still have the pack of zip ties in the back that we used on him before."

"Kidnap him?"

He shrugs, a small smile toying with his lips. "Only until he agrees to be ours."

"Coercion?"

"Seems as good a plan as any."

A laugh escapes my lips. "That may work. We could tease him, play with him, keeping him right on the edge of release until he concedes."

"Now that is a devious plan."

I lick my lips with the possibilities. Although I know it's something we'd never actually do, I let my mind wander with the potential.

"I doubt it would take long," Kingston says. "He'll never be able to resist your perfect mouth."

Just then his eyes lower to my lips, and the familiar tingle that's always present around him comes alive.

Not for the first time since Max turned us down, I allow myself the luxury of picturing a happiness with just Kingston and me. Even in my head it doesn't work. I know deep down that it's the three of us or nothing at all.

"Let's go inside and watch a movie," Kingston says rather than making a suggestion of what my lips should be doing.

We're back to waiting, back to keeping our distance until something can be decided with Max.

I let him take my hand when we hit the concrete, and I refuse to let go even when he reaches to push the button for my floor on the elevator panel.

"Maybe we can watch that new Sandra Bullock movie," I suggest when the elevator stops.

"No," is his only response.

No matter how many times I've tried, I can't get him interested in chick flicks.

"Why?" I whine. "She's a serious badass in that movie. The ratings are phenom—"

We both stop dead in our tracks at the sight of the man sitting against my front door. Even with his head lowered, forehead resting on his knees, we know who it is.

My throat is an instant desert because just hours ago Max rejected us. Told us in no certain terms that there will never be a partnership between the three of us, yet, here he sits, huddled against my door like he's been waiting a lifetime to get back to us.

I take another step closer to him, but Kingston grabs my arm, keeping me from running to him. When I look over at him, I don't fully understand what he's trying to tell me with the fiery set of his eyes and mouth, but it's clear he wants me to wait. So, I do. I stand mere feet from the second half of my heart when all I want to do is throw myself at him and beg him to realize that he wants the same things we do.

"Max?" Kingston grunts.

When the man in question lifts his head, his eyes are rimmed red with exhaustion. His throat works on a swallow, but he doesn't say a thing.

"Please let me go to him," I beg Kingston, but he doesn't soften his grip on my hand.

Silently, Max stands, taking a frustrating moment to wipe his hands down the back of his jeans like the floor is so dirty he can't wait to be rid of the filth.

It's a stall tactic, one that only serves to ramp up the tension filling the already narrow hallway.

"You left me thirteen years ago," Max begins, and I feel Kingston stiffen beside me. "You walked out and never looked back, and when I went to California after finding out that Mia told you I died, I found a broken man. Kingston Jacks was no longer in the Marine Corps. He'd been replaced with the shell of a man who drank more than anyone should, and the only thing that brought you out of that despair was getting deployed again. It took six years before you stopped spending your free time drinking your pain away, and I was the bitter son of a bitch that let it continue. I felt justified in letting you wallow in grief. It was more emotion than you showed when you left me. It was so fucking easy for you to walk out of my life, to turn your back on what we had. And now? Now, you want me to drop everything, give up on my sister and her needs to fall right back into your bed."

"Max," I whisper, the tears in my eyes clear in the shattered tone of my voice.

He doesn't look at me.

"Maybe we should go inside," I offer, but Kingston holds his hand up to silence me.

I know this has been a long time coming but hashing all of this out in the hallway where any one of my neighbors could have their ears to their doors isn't the place for it.

"Let him finish."

"I could easily do that. I could fall to my knees and continue to worship you exactly the way I did in high school but to what end? I don't see a future where you don't turn your back on me again. And what about Jasmine? She deserves better than the sight of you walking away when you decide there's something better than her."

My hand clenches, and I don't realize how hard I'm squeezing Kingston's hand until his thumb brushes over the back of mine.

I've run this scenario over in my head. I've thought about the aftermath of not having them, of having them only temporarily, but I came to the conclusion that not having them at all would be more painful than the heartbreak that Max seems to be predicting.

Is this love? Is this what it means to care for someone so deeply that you're able to face the uncertainty of the future so long as you can have something in the moment? Or is that stupidity? Is it a selfish, immature choice to take what you can get for now?

"I won't leave again," Kingston says.

"I don't believe you." Max licks his dry lips as his head shakes back and forth. "I can't survive you again."

"What can I do? What can I say to make you believe me?"

Kingston releases my hand to walk closer to Max. The other man takes a step back until he crashes against my apartment door. A shuttering breath escapes his lungs as his eyes squeeze tight. My own chest constricts when Kingston lifts his huge hand to stroke down the side of Max's wet cheek.

"Let me prove it to you. Let me show you how much I love you. How much I love her."

"I want that so much," Max whispers, "but I can't trust it. I can't trust your promises. You promised me forever when we were kids. Long before we became lovers, you told me we'd be best friends until we die."

"And that hasn't changed," Kingston assures him brushing his lips over the scruff on Max's jaw.

Another sob racks Max as Kingston wraps him in his arm, moving him to the side so I can unlock the door. Holding the door open until they pass by, I'm left standing to watch them as Kingston embraces his friend, comforting him.

"Jasmine," Max whispers when I go to leave the living room.

Only the feelings of dread have already begun to settle inside of me. Kingston just confessed that he loves me, and as much as that warms me, the sight of them together again is making me feel like an outsider.

"Come here," Max begs, and when I turn to look at him, I find both men with a hand reached out in my direction.

"I can't do this." I hold my hands up by my head and take another step back.

Kingston frowns while Max just looks resolved. I don't think we'll ever all be on the same page at the same time.

"How can you go from hating him and spitting your revenge in one second to crying on his chest the next? You said back at the clubhouse that we weren't going to be together, yet two hours later, you're here."

"Max lied at the clubhouse. He didn't want to turn us down. He felt like he had to," Kingston explains. "He never takes a step back to assess what it is that will make him happy."

"Only today I did just that," Max says as he wipes his tears away. "I don't want to go another day without this."

"Without him, you mean," I clarify. "It's clear you guys are meant to be together. Stop."

I back away more when Kingston stands to cross the room toward me.

"I don't want to be placated. I'm not saying this to get attention or assurances that I'm a part of this. It's clear that you guys are destined for a future."

Kingston chuckles, crossing the room even though I'm warding him off with my hands up. Before Kingston can reach me, Max is also standing and making his way across the room.

"Have you not been listening?" Max asks as he circles around me.

"Have you not felt the way you make us burn?" Kingston adds.

"That's just s-sex, nothing more," I whisper.

Things would've been a lot simpler had this not carried on past what we were doing at the club. *Hale-ish* seems like a lifetime ago. It was before the trauma of Mia's abduction, before the soft kisses and lingering looks. It was before the casing around my heart cracked open enough for not one but for both of these men to infiltrate and set up camp.

"Please don't," I beg when Max presses against my back as Kingston swarms my front.

"This isn't just about sex," Max lies. "It hasn't been about that for a long time now."

"We can spend the rest of our lives without touching each other in that way if it will prove to you that this is about our hearts and our future, not just the shit below the waist," Kingston says.

Both Max and I laugh, his full of doubt, mine humorless with Kingston's impossible promise.

"I'll tell you the same thing I told Max. Let me prove it to you. Let him prove it to you."

"Your heart is already hurting, sweet girl. Let us convince you that right here with us is exactly where you're supposed to be."

I can't believe how convincing they are. I gave them an out, and neither one of them is taking it. My heart slams an uneven tempo in my chest with everything that this could mean.

"If you break my heart, I'll have my dad break your faces," I vow.

Chapter 40

Max

"I thought we weren't going to have sex," Jasmine moans as my fingers slip into the front of her jeans.

I haven't even made contact with that sweet spot between her legs, and she's already writhing against us.

"We can stop," Kingston lies, his mouth sweeping kisses against her neck. "Watch that Sandra Bullock movie you wanted to see."

"Or," I begin, dipping my fingers a couple of inches lower, "we can see where this goes."

"I kn-know where it's going," she stutters as Kingston pinches one of her nipples over her clothes.

"And where is that?" he challenges.

"To my room. To the bed."

"Maybe we'll fuck you right here on the living room floor," I predict as my fingers slide through the slickness of her desire.

Her mouth is arguing, but her body is singing a different tune.

"Okay," she agrees with an aggressive nod of her head. "Here's fine."

"I don't want you to do something you don't want to d—"

"I want it," she assures Kingston.

"Good thing, because that tight little ass of yours keeps rubbing all over my cock, and I don't think I'd be able to stop even if you were begging me to." It's a lie. She can always say no, I just know that she won't. Her body is primed for us, and the heady scent of her arousal is infiltrating my nose and making me want to bend her over right here and take what I need from her body.

"Let's go to the room," Kingston urges.

"Here's fine," Jasmine repeats.

"What we need is in the other room," he argues, nipping hard on her earlobe until she moans again.

"We don't need a bed," she insists. "Take my clothes off."

Kingston grabs her hands when she reaches for the front button of her jeans.

"I'm not going to fuck your ass without lube, Jasmine."

"Oh, God," she whimpers.

My cock is a steel pipe in my jeans, and completely on board with what he's suggesting. She complains with a whine when I pull my fingers free from the front of her pants.

"Go on." I slap her ass to get her to move toward the bedroom.

"Don't," Kingston warns when she begins to pull her shirt off as she walks in that direction. "We get to unwrap you."

"A belated Christmas present?" I smile at Kingston. "It's exactly what I've always wanted."

We prowl, stalking her like prey until we get into her room.

"What are you waiting for?" Jasmine asks as we both stand, content with just watching the breathless rise and fall of her chest. "Unwrap me."

"If you don't, I will," I warn him. My cock is begging to be released, and I've never been one to ignore his needs.

"Maybe we should let her unwrap herself?"

Her hands reach for the hem of her shirt, but they stop just short of pulling the fabric up. She's waiting for his command.

"Just so long as she gets naked," I insist.

"You first," he says as he turns in my direction. "Strip."

I bite my lip to keep from smiling, but my hands automatically move into action at his command. He's potent, a powerful force, and one I've never been able to resist. It if weren't for the work Dominic needed me to do earlier, I would've run after them sooner. How I had the gumption to walk out of that room in the first place is beyond me. It broke my heart to check both my guest bedroom and his, only to find them empty.

"Someone's excited," Kingston says as he steps forward and clasps my cock in his strong hand. "Don't move."

When I turn my head toward Jasmine, I find her two steps closer to us and a frown on her perfect lips.

"How could you ever have wanted to give this up?" Kingston challenges her.

"I didn't," she promises. "I just don't want to get hurt."

"Oh, we're going to hurt you. Don't ever doubt that." His hand works my dick with an almost leisurely stroke. It's enough to get me excited but will never be enough to get me off. "We're going to ram our cocks so deep down your throat, you'll gag. We're going to slam inside of that tight cunt so hard you'll whimper from the intrusion. That ass of yours will never be the same when I'm done with you."

"Promise?" The one-word, breathless plea is enough to make him release my cock and turn toward her.

"Max, get her naked."

I don't waste a second. My hands move into action, pulling her shirt over her head before flicking open the clasp on her bra. I don't even take a second to admire her luscious tits before moving to the button and zipper on her jeans.

"You never were one to enjoy the anticipation," Kingston says with a chuckle. "Go slow."

Jasmine whimpers again when my hands touch her softer, the fevered rush from before dissipating like smoke from a campfire.

"Please," Jasmine begs when I leave her panties on her hips and push down her jeans by themselves.

Thankful she's wearing boots with a zipper rather than intricate laces. I get them off next, her jeans following close behind.

"Look how perfect she is," Kingston praises. "And to think we get to spend the rest of our lives pleasing her. How the fuck did we ever get so lucky?"

I ignore the sentiment, the unspoken vow in his words. If I focus too long on the future, I won't have the energy they both deserve from me.

"So perfect," I agree as I lift my mouth to her furled nipple.

"Did I give you permission to do that?" Kingston growls as he slaps a heavy hand on my ass.

I've played this game before, so I anticipated the blow. He was counting on it since her delicate nipple is clamped between my teeth. He promised to hurt her, but real pain, an injury bad enough to draw blood would never be his intention.

"You're supposed to share." Jasmine pouts as I pull my mouth away.

"I'll share." When I turn, I see fire glinting in Kingston's eyes. "Why don't you both come share my cock?"

As if he were offering a sip of water in a decade long drought, we both drop to our knees, crowding his front.

Jasmine pops open the button on his jeans while I work the laces open on his combat boots. I shove the idea of letting him fuck me while wearing full gear to the back of my mind, so I can revisit it later.

"Lift," I insist as I tug on one boot. Before long, both boots are off, and Jasmine has shoved down his jeans and boxers in one go. Clearly, she's as eager for presents as I am.

"Do we go slow with this, too?" she asks as her tongue makes the first swipe on the underside of his thick cock.

Kingston moans his response, but when she only plants teasing licks and kisses to his shaft, he takes command, wrapping his hand in her hair and pulling her head down to take as much as she can. She gags when he hits the back of her throat, but that only makes his cock jerk harder.

"Don't forget to share," he says as he pulls her off. She gasps with the allowed intake of air as he positions his cock at my lips. I don't have to be instructed. I know from the look in his eye that I need to relax my throat and let him take what he needs, and fuck if I don't love every damned second of giving it to him.

"That's it," he praises as he slides down my throat. "You always knew how to please me."

Jasmine's hand runs the length of my spine, and I can tell by the skipping movement that she's eager for her next chance. However, when she lifts her hand to grope his nuts, Kingston pulls away from both of us completely.

"What's wrong?" Jasmine asks when he takes a step back.

He rips his shirt over his head, and I can't help the laugh that slips past my swollen lips.

"Nothing, sweet girl. He was close to coming," I explain. I could tell by the burst of pre-cum he rewarded me with that he was on edge.

"On the bed, all fours," he snaps when he finds me grinning at him.

He hates to lose control, and there's no harder hit to a man's ego than coming too soon.

Jasmine scrambles for the bed, lifting her pert ass in the air. She's on display, and the sight of her pink slit makes my mouth water to taste her.

"Sheer perfection," Kingston says as he takes a step closer to her.

I grunt my agreement, my hand snaking down my abs to reach for my aching dick. I need her like never before, but when she looks over her shoulder at us, Kingston reaches for me instead.

"Thank you for coming back to us," he whispers against my mouth before his tongue slips inside and wrecks me.

My hands are greedy as I run them over every inch of his body I can reach. It isn't until Jasmine moans that I pull away.

"Naughty girl," Kingston chides as he looks at her while licking his lips.

She's angled herself so she can see us better, and two fingers are toying with the delicate flesh between her legs. Her white teeth are sunk hard into her lower lip as she tries to keep from moaning.

"What do we do with naughty girls, Max?"

"We fuck them until they behave."

"Get on the bed and let her sink down on that massive cock of yours," Kingston instructs as he makes his way over to the bedside drawer.

Faster than lightning, Jasmine pulls her fingers from her core and is already shifting to the side, so I can lie down. In the next breath, she's angling my dick upward and lowering her sexy body down.

"Fuck," I groan when she takes me to the root.

Kingston is the only person I've been inside of bare, and it was the best thing I've ever felt, but she's giving him a run for his money.

"God," she hisses when Kingston dribbles the cold lube over her ass.

It pools on my nuts, and even though it wasn't needed due to her already drenched state, it changes the glide of her on my cock.

"Don't stop," Kingston insists when the motion of her hips stop.

"What's he doing?" I ask, already having an idea of what the moan she just released means.

"He's fingering my ass," she pants.

As much as I feel she wants to obey him, she's struggling with taking his fingers and bouncing on me, so I show her some mercy. Gripping her hips and spreading my legs higher, I use the strength in my abs to ram inside of her.

"That's the hottest thing I've ever seen. The way your cock is owning her... mmm."

Clenching my teeth, I slow the movements of my hips. "Shut up."

I can tell Kingston knows exactly what's going on when he laughs.

"Who's close to coming now?" he teases.

Just then fingers from his free hand skate over the lube on my balls until they're pressing against my own ass.

"You'll end this now," I warn when he dips inside to the first knuckle.

I whimper when he pulls his fingers away, hating the loss of him but appreciating the reprieve.

"I'm ready," Jasmine assures him as I feel the brush of his digits on the other side of that thin membrane separating me from him.

"You sure?" He moves deeper inside of her. "That's only three fingers."

I moan for her, knowing just how good three of his fingers feel. I also know that four fingers would be closer to what he's planning on replacing them with.

"Promise," she heaves. "Come fuck me. I want to feel both of you inside of me."

I growl when my cock jerks at her filthy words. As if knowing what's going to happen, Kingston shifts her weight until my dick is barely inside of her, then he squeezes my shaft to the point of pain. My back molars grind together at the agony of his grip, but at the same time, I'm grateful.

"Okay," I tell him, so he'll let go. "Give the girl what she wants."

"What we all want," he reminds us as he climbs on the bed, crouching behind her.

He pushes her down until she's fully impaled on my dick before he breaches her other hole.

"Fuck, fuck, fuck," she gasps when he slides inside. "I'm so full."

"Just relax," I tell her as I press my lips to her throat. "Let your body stretch around us."

"Goddamn," Kingston hisses when he shifts back a few inches only to delve several more inside. "You better be able to reach her clit, Max, and you may want to do it quickly."

My lower abdomen is soaked with her juices and remnants of the lube, and I'm grateful for the ease I'm able to reach her clit. There isn't enough room between our bodies with Kingston's weight on her, but I'm able to pinch her clit between two knuckles.

"Mmm," she moans, and it seems like it may be enough. "More."

I don't know if she wants to get fucked harder or if she wants me to increase the pressure on her clit, so I offer her both. I lift my hips, pounding into her when Kingston shifts backward. When he rams forward, it magnifies my pinching fingers, and before long she's so lost in it, she stops making noise. Her mouth hangs open. Her eyes roll back before the lids flutter closed. I feel the orgasm in her limbs, in the shake of her legs and the tremble of her arms near my shoulders long before her pussy clamps down on my dick.

"Goddammit," Kingston hisses just moments before I feel his cock jerk inside of her.

Not one to be outdone, my own cock jerks with release, long spurts echoing the rippling clench of her pussy.

I somehow see stars in the pitch black when my own eyes close. The strength of my orgasm has a headache threatening at the base of my skull.

"You going to answer that?" Jasmine whisper against my neck.

"What?"

"Your phone has gone off twice in the last three minutes," she explains.

I plan to let it go to voicemail, seeing as we need a little time to come down from this mountainous high, but when it silences, it begins ringing again.

Jasmine whimpers when Kingston eases out of her. When he's standing, he scoops her up, my still half-hard cock slapping me in the stomach.

"I'll clean our princess. You answer your damn phone. Round two in thirty minutes."

Jasmine chuckles as he carries her to the bathroom while I reach for my phone. It rings again before I can get it out of my jeans pocket.

SCOOTER flashing on the screen makes my blood run cold.

"What's wrong?" I ask as soon as the call connects.

"It's Mia." He sounds frantic, his breath soughing loudly through the mic as if he's just finished running a marathon. "She's gone. We can't find her anywhere."

Need more Cerberus MC? Grab Scooter's story HERE!

Social Media Links

[FB Author Page](#)
[FB Author Group](#)
[Twitter](#)
[Instagram](#)
[BookBub](#)
Reader Email Share: [HERE](#)

[Newsletter](#)

OTHER BOOKS FROM MARIE JAMES

Standalones
Crowd Pleaser
Macon
We Said Forever
More Than a Memory

Cole Brothers SERIES
Love Me Like That
Teach Me Like That

Hale Series
Coming to Hale
Begging for Hale
Hot as Hale
To Hale and Back
Hale Series Box Set

Cerberus MC
Kincaid: Cerberus MC Book 1
Kid: Cerberus MC Book 2
Shadow: Cerberus MC Book 3
Dominic: Cerberus MC Book 4
Snatch: Cerberus MC Book 5

Lawson: Cerberus MC Book 6
Hound: Cerberus MC Book 7
Griffin: Cerberus MC Book 8
Samson: Cerberus MC Book 9
Tug: Cerberus MC Book 10
Cerberus MC Box Set 1
Cerberus MC Box Set 2

Ravens Ruin MC
Desperate Beginnings: Prequel (Book 1)
(Not a romance, but gives all of the back history on the club)
Book 2: Sins of the Father
Book 3: Luck of the Devil
Book 4: Dancing with the Devil

MM Romance
Grinder
Taunting Tony

Made in United States
Orlando, FL
26 June 2025